W9-BEI-960

Tilly's diary:

Okay, here I am, halfway up a Scottish mountain, with a man I'd never met before this morning. It's funny to think that this time last night I'd never even heard of Campbell, and now it seems as if I've known him forever. And tonight we're going to sleep together…well, not sleep together—except, of course, we will be sleeping. Oh, you know what I mean.

Where was I? Oh, yes, Campbell… You should have seen him making me abseil down that cliff—two cliffs! Talk about competitive! And he's not exactly chatty. I've never met a man who talks so little about himself. Still, he's got that steely eyed thing going that's quite exciting when he's not pushing you down a cliff. Anyway, he wasn't so bad this afternoon. In fact, he was really quite nice—especially the last few miles. And now he's making me supper. I ought to offer to help, but I really don't think I've got the energy to get out of the tent. Perhaps if I just close my eyes for a moment, and then I'll go and give him a hand….

Dear Reader,

It's hard to believe this is my fiftieth book! It seems hardly any time since the excitement of seeing my first book in print. The thrill is still there with every book, but *Last-Minute Proposal* will always be a special one for me, especially coinciding as it does with my fiftieth birthday—and, yes, there will be a party! Looking back at fifty heroes and fifty heroines, I realize they were all favorites when I was writing them, but some have stayed with me more than others, so that even nearly twenty years since I was writing their story I'm thinking about where they are now and what they're doing.

I've got a feeling Tilly and Campbell will long be favorites, too, perhaps because I could identify so much with Tilly—with her love of food, her insecurity about her figure and her fear of abseiling. The opening scene was written entirely from my own experience. I, too, have hung off a cliff whimpering, "Don't let me go!"—although I'm ashamed to admit that Tilly is a lot braver than I was! Campbell has his own challenge to face, and that's just as difficult for him. But we all learn by stepping outside our comfort zones, and Tilly and Campbell both discover that having to do something they really don't want to do ends up being the best thing that ever happened to them.

I hope you'll enjoy this book as much as I enjoyed writing it!

Jessica

x

JESSICA HART
Last-Minute Proposal

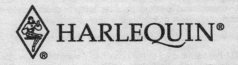

TORONTO • NEW YORK • LONDON
AMSTERDAM • PARIS • SYDNEY • HAMBURG
STOCKHOLM • ATHENS • TOKYO • MILAN • MADRID
PRAGUE • WARSAW • BUDAPEST • AUCKLAND

If you purchased this book without a cover you should be aware that this book is stolen property. It was reported as "unsold and destroyed" to the publisher, and neither the author nor the publisher has received any payment for this "stripped book."

ISBN-13: 978-0-373-17544-4
ISBN-10:   0-373-17544-2

LAST-MINUTE PROPOSAL

First North American Publication 2008.

Copyright © 2008 by Jessica Hart.

All rights reserved. Except for use in any review, the reproduction or utilization of this work in whole or in part in any form by any electronic, mechanical or other means, now known or hereafter invented, including xerography, photocopying and recording, or in any information storage or retrieval system, is forbidden without the written permission of the publisher, Harlequin Enterprises Limited, 225 Duncan Mill Road, Don Mills, Ontario, Canada M3B 3K9.

This is a work of fiction. Names, characters, places and incidents are either the product of the author's imagination or are used fictitiously, and any resemblance to actual persons, living or dead, business establishments, events or locales is entirely coincidental.

This edition published by arrangement with Harlequin Books S.A.

® and TM are trademarks of the publisher. Trademarks indicated with ® are registered in the United States Patent and Trademark Office, the Canadian Trade Marks Office and in other countries.

www.eHarlequin.com

Printed in U.S.A.

Jessica Hart was born in West Africa, and has suffered from itchy feet ever since. She has traveled and worked around the world in a wide variety of interesting but very lowly jobs, all of which provided inspiration on which to draw when it comes to the settings and plots of her stories. Now she lives a rather more settled existence in York, U.K., where she has been able to pursue her interest in history, although she still yearns sometimes for wider horizons. If you'd like to know more about Jessica, visit her Web site, www.jessicahart.co.uk.

"RITA® Award-winning author Jessica Hart never disappoints her readers with her spellbinding and sophisticated stories, brimming with warmth, wit, drama and romance."
—*CataRomance*

"Jessica Hart is a marvel."
—*Romantic Times BOOKreviews*

Jessica Hart is "smart, sassy and sophisticated."
—*CataRomance*

For all those readers whose support
over the last fifty books has meant so much.
This one is for you, with thanks.

CHAPTER ONE

'DON'T let me go!'

Tilly's voice rose to a shrill whisper as she grabbed Campbell Sanderson's neck and hung on for dear life. He was rock-solid and smelt reassuringly clean and masculine. And he was the only thing standing between her and the bottom of a cliff.

Typical. The closest she had been to a bloke for ages and she was too terrified to enjoy it.

Campbell reached up to prise her hands away. 'I've no intention of letting you go,' he said irritably. 'I'm going to hold the rope while you lower yourself down. It's perfectly simple. All you have to do is lean back and trust me.'

'And how many women over the centuries have heard *that* line?' snapped Tilly, clamping her arms determinedly back in place the moment he released them. 'It's all very well for you to talk about trust, but you're not the one being asked to dangle over an abyss with only a thin rope between you and certain death!'

One thing was sure—certain death was awaiting her twin brothers, who were responsible for getting her into this mess. She was going to kill them the moment she got off this sodding hillside.

If she ever got off this hillside.

Tilly risked a glance at Campbell. It was odd to be so close to a perfect stranger at all, let alone clasping him quite so fervently, and she examined him with a strange, detached part of her mind that was prepared to do anything other than think about abseiling down the sheer cliff face.

He had glacier-green eyes that were the coldest and most implacable she had ever seen, close-cropped hair and an expression of profound impatience. Of course, that might just be inspired by her, Tilly had to acknowledge, but she had a feeling it was habitual. He seemed the impatient type. Tilly was the last person to deny that appearances could be deceptive, but there was something about the austere angles of his face and the ruthless set of his mouth that made her think that here was a prime example of 'what you see is what you get'.

And what you got in the case of Campbell Sanderson was a very tough customer indeed.

'How can I trust you?' she demanded, without releasing her limpet-like grip. 'I don't know anything about you.'

Campbell sucked in an exasperated breath. 'I don't know you either,' he pointed out crisply. 'So why would I want to drop you down a cliff, especially with a television camera trained on me? Or hadn't you noticed they're filming you right now?'

'Of course I've noticed! Why do you think I'm whispering?'

Tilly's arms were aching with the effort of holding on to him. Her feet were braced just over the lip of the cliff, but she could feel gravity pulling her weight backwards.

And, let's face it, it was a substantial weight to be pulled. Why, oh, why hadn't she stuck to any of her diets? Tilly wondered wildly. This was a punishment to her for not subsisting on lettuce leaves for the past thirty years.

Campbell glanced at the distant cameras in disbelief. 'They're miles away! Of course they can't hear you, but they can see you.

They've got a socking great zoom on that camera and it's pointed straight at you so, for God's sake, pull yourself together!' he told her sharply. 'You're making yourself look ridiculous.'

And him by association.

'Better to be ridiculous than splattered all over the bottom of this cliff!'

A muscle was jumping in his cheek and his jaw looked suspiciously set. 'For a start, this is not a cliff,' he said with the kind of restraint that suggested that he was only hanging on to his temper with extreme difficulty. 'It's barely twenty feet to the bottom there and, as I keep telling you, you're not going to fall. You're on a secure rope, and you can let yourself down slowly. Even if you did lose control, I've got hold of the rope and I'd stop you dropping.'

'You might not be able to,' said Tilly, not at all convinced. 'That rope's awfully fine. I can't believe it'll hold my weight.'

'Of course it will,' he said impatiently. 'This rope could hold a hippopotamus.'

'Now, I wonder what made you think of a hippo,' Tilly said bitterly.

She wished Campbell hadn't mentioned the zoom on that camera. It was probably trained on her bottom right now. Unsure of quite what 'a day in the hills' involved, but fairly sure it would mean getting cold, she had squeezed herself into her old skiing salopettes, bought in a burst of enthusiasm soon after she had met Olivier and was at least two sizes smaller. Now her big red bottom would be filling the screen down there, and the television crew would all be having a good laugh.

Tilly had a dark suspicion that had been the idea all along.

'Who thought up this show in the first place?' she demanded, fear and humiliation giving her voice a treacherous wobble, but at least talking took her mind off the void beneath her.

'God knows,' said Campbell, thinking that a deep longing to be elsewhere was probably all that he and Tilly had in common.

'I bet they were sitting around in some bar or wherever television types congregate, and someone said, "Hey, I know, let's make a programme where we make fat people look absolutely ridiculous!"'

'If that were the case, all the contestants would be fat and, in fact, none of us are,' he pointed out impatiently.

'*I* am.'

'Not noticeably,' said Campbell, although now she came to mention it, the figure clutching him was definitely on the voluptuous side.

He had been too focused on the task in hand to notice at first, which was perhaps just as well. Under other circumstances, he would have enjoyed the situation. He was only human, after all, and he certainly wasn't going to object if a lush-bodied woman chose to press herself against him. Sadly, however many points Matilda Jenkins might score on the physical front, she was losing a lot more with all this carry-on about a simple abseil.

'Your theory is nonsense, in fact,' he told her. 'None of the other novices are the slightest bit overweight.'

Tilly thought back to the meeting that morning, where they had met their three rival pairs who had also made it through from the first round. Much as it might go against the grain, she had to admit that Campbell was right.

Leanne had a perfect figure, for instance. Tilly had noticed her straight away as a possible kindred spirit. She was the only other contestant wearing make-up and looked about as happy to be there as Tilly was. It turned out that Leanne was a beautician, blonde and very pretty, and, almost as much as her figure, Tilly had envied her partner, a gregarious outdoor sports instructor called Roger who had all the latest equipment and was friendly and reassuring. The opposite of Campbell, in fact.

Leanne definitely wasn't fat, and nor were the other two girls. Defying the usual stereotypes, one of them was a capable-looking outdoorsy type who had been teamed with a medieval art historian raising money for the restoration of some cathedral's stained glass, and even he was downright skinny.

'Well, perhaps they thought it was funny to make us *all* look ridiculous,' Tilly conceded grudgingly, reluctant to let go of her theory completely. She managed a mirthless laugh, no small achievement when you were teetering on the edge of a sheer drop—and she didn't care what Campbell said about twenty feet, it felt like the side of the Grand Canyon to her. 'Ha, ha.'

'More than likely,' said Campbell tersely, 'but, since we've all agreed to take part, we're not in a position to complain about it now.'

Further along the rock face, he could see his three competitors preparing their partners for the abseil. There were three other beginners in Tilly's position, chosen for their complete lack of experience with anything remotely connected with outdoor activities, but they seemed to be getting on with what they had to do without any of the drama Matilda Jenkins seemed determined to wring from the situation.

He blew out a breath. There were better things to be doing on a bright, cold Saturday in the Highlands. A brisk wind was pushing the clouds past the sun, sending shadows scudding over the hills around them, and the air smelt of peat and heather. It would be a great day for a climb, or just to walk off the restlessness that had plagued him so often recently.

Instead of which, he had a hysterical woman on his hands. Campbell didn't care how lush her body was, how appealing her perfume. He would rather be behind enemy lines again than cope with a scene of the kind Matilda Jenkins was evidently all too capable of creating.

Why had he ever let Keith talk him into this? Good PR, indeed! How the hell could it be good PR for Manning's Chief Executive to be seen being strangled by a panicky woman at the top of a drop so short you could practically step down to the bottom?

And this was only the beginning, Campbell reminded himself darkly. He had to get the bloody woman down this rock face, across the hill, into the valley and across the river at the bottom before the others, or they wouldn't get through to the next round, and if they didn't do that, they wouldn't win the competition.

And Campbell Sanderson didn't do not winning.

Tempting as it was to just push her over the edge and lower her to the bottom, Campbell reluctantly discarded that option. He was prepared to bet that Jenkins had a scream that would be heard across the border in England. The noise would be appalling, and she had a surprisingly strong grip, too. He wouldn't put it past her to try and drag him back with her, and they would end up wrestling and making themselves look even more ridiculous than they did already.

No, he was going to have to talk her down.

Drawing a breath, Campbell forced patience into his voice.

'Come along, Jenkins, you're losing your grip here,' he told her. 'The way I see it, you've got two choices. You can let me pull you back on to the top here and admit defeat, sure, but are you really prepared to let down the charity you're doing this for in the first place? They're going to be pretty disappointed when you tell them that you bottled out because you were too chicken to do a simple abseil. They'll be counting on you winning lots of money for them. What is your charity, anyway?' he asked casually.

'The local hospice,' Tilly muttered. She wished he hadn't brought that up. Of course she ought to be thinking about the hospice and everything they had done for her mother, and for Jack. She set her teeth.

'Great cause,' he commented. 'There'll be lots of people rooting for you to do well, then.'

'Oh, yes, pile on the emotional blackmail, why don't you?' she said bitterly.

'I'm just telling it like it is,' said Campbell with a virtuous air. 'One option is to disappoint all those people, not to mention the television company who have set up this challenge. The other is to take your arms from round my neck, lean back against the tension of the rope and walk slowly backwards down the rock face. It'll be over in a minute, and you'll feel great once you've done it.'

Tilly doubted that very much. More than likely, she wouldn't be in a position to feel anything ever again.

'Isn't there another option?'

'We could spend the rest of our lives up here with our arms around each other, I suppose, but I don't imagine that's an option you want to consider.'

'Oh, I don't know…' said Tilly, playing for time.

The worrying thing was that it wasn't actually *that* unappealing an option. Obviously, she hardly knew him, and he did seem rather cross, but on the other hand there were worse fates than spending the rest of your life holding on to a body like Campbell Sanderson's. He might not be the friendliest or best-looking man she had ever met, but Tilly had to admit there was something about that cold-eyed, stern-mouthed, lean-jawed look.

If only he wasn't so determined to make her lean back over the void. Why couldn't he be intent on whisking her away for a fabulous weekend in Paris instead?

'Come on, Jenkins, make up your mind.' Impatience was creeping back into Campbell's voice. He glanced along to where the other contestants were almost at the bottom of the rock face. 'We haven't got all day here. It's time to stop messing around and just get on with it.'

Tilly sighed. Obviously he wasn't keen on the clinging together for eternity option. She couldn't really blame him. If

Campbell Sanderson was going to spend the rest of his life with anyone, it certainly wouldn't be with a panicky, overweight cook.

'You'll be absolutely fine,' the production assistant had reassured her when breaking the news that her original partner had had to drop out. She'd lowered her voice confidentially. 'Campbell Sanderson is ex-special forces, I heard,' she'd whispered enviously. 'You couldn't be in better hands.'

Tilly looked at Campbell's hands on the rope. They were strong and square and very capable. The sort of hands that would ease the strap of a sexy nightdress off your shoulder with just the right amount of *frisson*-inducing brushing of warm fingers. The sort of hands that under any other circumstances it would be a real pleasure to find yourself between, in fact.

More importantly, the sort of hands that wouldn't drop or fumble with a rope when you were dangling on the end of it.

'Jenkins…' he said warningly, and Tilly dragged herself back to the matter in hand.

'All right, all right…'

She was going to have to do it, Tilly realised. She had to do it for her mother and for everyone who needed the care she had had, but Tilly's stomach still turned sickeningly at the prospect.

Trust me, Campbell had said. She risked a glance into his face and saw him in extraordinary detail. The pale green eyes, the dark brows drawn together in a forbidding frown, that mouth clamped in an exasperated line… Funny how she hadn't noticed him in the same way when they'd been introduced.

Then, he had simply struck her as taciturn. Now, he seemed cool, competent, unsmiling. She could just see him in a balaclava, parachuting behind the lines to blow up a few tanks before tea. He clearly wasn't the type to fool around. Unlike some males of her acquaintance, Campbell Sanderson wouldn't pretend to drop her for a lark, just so he could chortle at her squeals of terror. No, he would do exactly what he said he would do.

In return, all she had to do was lean back, walk down the cliff. And trust him.

Tilly drew a breath. She was going to have to do *something*.

Very, very cautiously, she loosened her hold on Campbell's neck.

'If I do it will you stop calling me by my surname?' she asked.

'Whatever you want,' said Campbell, one eye on the other competitors, who were already packing up and getting ready to head down the hillside. 'Just do it.'

'OK,' said Tilly bravely. 'Let's get on with it then.'

In spite of her best resolution, it took a couple of attempts before she had the nerve to let go of his neck completely and put her hands on the rope instead.

'Good,' said Campbell, and she was ashamed of the tiny glow of warmth she felt at his approval.

He explained what she needed to do. 'Off you go, then,' he said briskly.

Tilly inched her way back to the edge. 'You won't let me fall?' Her voice was wavering on the verge of panic again and Campbell looked straight into her eyes.

'Trust me,' he said again.

'Right,' said Tilly and, taking a deep breath, she leant backwards over the empty air.

It would be too much to say that she enjoyed her abseil, but the hardest part was that first moment of leaning into the void, and once she was making her way down the cliff, gradually letting out the rope, it didn't seem quite so terrifying. Campbell was at the top, letting out the rope as she went, and very quickly, it seemed, her feet touched the grass and she was collapsing into an untidy heap.

The next moment, Campbell had abseiled down in two easy

jumps and was gathering up the equipment. 'Come on,' he said briskly, barely sparing a glance at Tilly, who was still sprawled on the grass and recovering from the trauma of her descent. 'We're behind.'

Reluctantly, Tilly hauled herself upright. Her legs felt distinctly wobbly but when she looked up at the rock face, she could see that it wasn't in fact that high. Campbell had been right, damn him.

'What now?' she asked.

'Now we have to get down and across the river, and we have to do it before the others, or we can't be sure of getting through to the next round.' Campbell coiled the last rope and stowed it away in his rucksack. 'Come on.'

He strode off, leaving Tilly to trot after him. 'Are you sure you're going the right way?' she asked a little breathlessly, and pointed over her shoulder. 'Everyone else has gone that way.'

'Which is why we're going *this* way,' said Campbell, not breaking his stride in the slightest. 'It's a tougher route, but much quicker.'

'How on earth do you know that?'

'I looked at a map this morning.'

Tilly stared at his back. 'Boy, you really do want to win, don't you?' Her father was the only person she knew with that kind of drive to win at any cost.

'Why are you here if you don't?' he countered. Just as her father would have done.

'I was tricked into it.' Tilly's blue eyes sparkled with remembered indignation. 'My twin brothers decided that it was time for me to get out of my rut and entered me in the competition. The first I knew of it was when people who work at the hospice started coming up to me and telling me how thrilled they were that I was taking part and what wonderful things they would be able to do with the money if I won. So I could hardly turn round then and say it was all a terrible mistake, could I?' she grumbled.

Campbell glanced down at her. Her heart-shaped face was pink with exertion and she was vainly trying to stop the breeze blowing the mass of curly brown hair into her eyes. She looked cross and ruffled and vibrant in her red ski-suit. It seemed a bizarre choice to wear for a weekend walking in the hills, but at least there was no chance of her getting lost. You could see her coming a mile away. Perhaps the television people had told her they wanted her to be noticeable—although it was hard to imagine *not* noticing her.

'Why not?' he asked. 'If you didn't want to do it, you could have just said so.'

Of course he *would* say that, thought Tilly. It was easy for people like Campbell Sanderson and her father, who only ever focused on one thing. They didn't worry about what other people would think or whether feelings would be hurt. They just said what they thought and did what they wanted and it never occurred to them to feel guilty about anything.

'It would have seemed so selfish,' she tried to explain. 'The hospice is a really special place. It was so awful when we knew my mother was dying. She was in pain, my brothers were very young, my stepfather was distraught... I was trying to hold things together but I didn't know what to do.'

The dark blue eyes were sad as she remembered that terrible time. 'I was so afraid of Mum dying,' she said. 'I don't know how any of us would have got through it without the hospice. It wasn't that we were any less bereft when she did die, but when she was there we were all calmer. They were so kind, not just to Mum, but to all of us. They helped us to understand what was happening, and accept it in a way we hadn't been able to do before.

'It was the same when my stepfather died,' said Tilly. 'It was still terrible, but we weren't so scared. I owe the hospice so much that I can't just back out. They were all so thrilled about the prospect of me taking part for them! If we win, they'll get the prize money, which would mean so much to them. They're building a new wing, so that other families can have the help and support we had. How could I turn round and say I wasn't going to try and help them after all?'

'There must be other ways of helping them,' Campbell pointed out.

'I volunteer in the shop,' said Tilly, 'but that isn't much of a sacrifice, is it?'

'It's more than most people do.'

'Maybe, but most people don't get a chance to win a huge donation to the charity of their choice either. If an opportunity like that comes along, it's virtually impossible to turn it down. I'd have felt worse than a piece of poo on your shoe if I had—as Harry and Seb no doubt worked out.'

'Harry and Seb?'

'My twin brothers,' Tilly told him without enthusiasm. 'This whole thing was their idea. They found out about the programme and took it upon themselves to enter me on my behalf. They sent in a photo and some spurious account of why I was so keen to take part—and then made sure everybody knew that I'd got through to the first round before I did so they were all lined up to lay on the emotional blackmail when Seb and Harry finally broke the news.

'At least, they didn't mean it as emotional blackmail,' she amended, wanting to be fair. 'Everyone at the hospice thought I wanted to take part and had just kept quiet in case I wasn't picked. So of course when my brothers told them that I was going to be on the programme, they were all delighted for me and kept telling me how proud Mum would have been if she knew what I was doing, which she would have been, of course.'

Tilly sighed. 'I *couldn't* disappoint them by telling them it was all a mistake, could I? It would have felt like letting Mum down, too.'

Campbell frowned as he headed across the hillside, cutting down from the track so that they had to leap between clumps of heather. At least, Tilly did. Campbell just carried on walking as if he were on a pavement. Tilly had never met anyone as surefooted. There was a kind of dangerous grace about the way he moved, and it made her feel even more of a lumbering walrus than she did normally.

He was obviously incredibly fit, too. Look at him—he wasn't even out of breath, thought Tilly, aggrieved, while she was puffing and panting and tripping over heather and generally making it obvious that she was extremely *un*fit.

'Why were your brothers so keen to get you on the programme?'

'They've got this bee in their bonnet that I'm in a rut,' puffed Tilly, struggling to keep up with him. 'I was thirty earlier this year and you'd think I was about to cash in my pension the way they're carrying on about my missed opportunities!'

'*Are* you in a rut?'

'If I am, it's a very comfortable one,' she said with an edge of defiance. 'I'm perfectly happy doing what I'm doing, and I haven't got time to worry about ruts. The boys only think that because they've been away at university, and they've got this idea that Allerby is boring—although I notice they don't mind coming back when they're short of money and in need of some good square meals,' she added tartly.

Of course, Campbell would probably think an attractive market town in North Yorkshire was boring, too. He didn't look like a provincial type. He would stand out like a tiger amongst a lot of fat, pampered pets in Allerby, for instance.

On the other hand, he didn't look like a true townie either. Tilly couldn't imagine him going to the theatre or sipping a cap-

puccino. His military background probably explained that
slightly dangerous edge to him, but then what was he doing here?

There was one easy way to find out.

'So what are *you* doing here? You don't seem the kind of
bloke who does things he doesn't want to do.'

'I seem to have ended up doing this,' said Campbell sourly.
'I'm Chief Executive of Manning Securities.'

'The sponsors of the show?'

'Exactly,' he said, without once breaking pace. 'Keith, my
PR Director, convinced me that the show would be good for
our image. Personally, I'd have thought it was more effective
just to give the money to charity, but Keith was adamant that
this would have a greater impact. It fitted with our ethos of corporate social responsibility and, as I didn't think I'd have to be
involved myself, I gave the go-ahead.'

'You look pretty involved now,' Tilly commented, and he
grunted a reluctant acknowledgement.

'Not out of choice. This is Keith's fault. He rang me yesterday morning, saying that one of the contestants had had to
withdraw because he'd broken his leg and that the production
team were desperate for a last-minute replacement with survival
skills.'

'That was Greg,' said Tilly. 'I met him last week when I learnt
I'd got through to this round. They said he was an experienced
Outward Bound instructor and a vegan, so I suppose they thought
he would make a good contrast with me. He seemed a nice enough
guy, but I can't tell you how relieved I was when I heard he'd
broken his leg. I thought I'd have the perfect reason to withdraw,
and then they partnered me with you!' Her expression was glum.

'Glad I was such a nice surprise!' said Campbell with a
touch of acid.

'Well, you can't pretend you're exactly thrilled at being
stuck with me for the next couple of days,' she pointed out.

'I'm not thrilled to be doing this at all,' he said. 'I'm moving to a new job in the States in a few weeks, so I've got better things to do than mess around with television challenges. But Keith is very committed to the project and, as he knows that I used to be in the forces, he was piling on the pressure to get me to agree to help out.'

'If you didn't want to do it, why didn't you just say so?' Tilly was delighted to be able to quote Campbell's words back to him. 'Aren't you military types trained not to give in to pressure?' she added innocently. 'You could have stuck to name, rank and serial number.'

Campbell shot her a look. 'Keith was a little cleverer than that. He talked a lot about how the programme wouldn't work if they didn't have the right number of contestants, and what a shame it would be if my last few weeks at Manning were re-membered for a failure.'

'Sounds like he knows just how to press all your buttons,' said Tilly, full of admiration for the unknown Keith. It was clear that he had his boss sussed. She had barely known Campbell for more than an hour, but even she could see that he was driven by the need to be the best. Any suggestion that he might be associated with failure would be like a red rag to a bull.

'He said it would just be a weekend with an amateur in the Highlands,' Campbell went on, darkly remembering how he had been misled. 'I didn't realise quite how much of an amateur you would be, I must admit.'

'Look at it from the television producers' point of view. Where's the fun if both of us know what we're doing? If you ask me, they want scenes like the one at the top of the cliff.'

'What cliff?'

'The one I abseiled down!'

'That little drop? You could have practically stepped down it!'

Tilly eyed him with dislike. 'So what's your charity?'

'What do you mean?'

'Everyone who's taking part is doing it for charity. So I'm doing it for the local hospice, and I think Greg was hoping to raise money for mountain rescue dogs or something. You must have some incentive to win.'

Campbell shrugged. 'Winning's enough for me,' he said. 'But I tell you what. My prize money will go to your hospice if we win, so they'll have a double donation.'

Double the money. Tilly thought about what that would mean to the hospice. 'Really?' she asked.

'Only if it gives *you* some incentive to hurry up,' he said astringently.

'I *am* hurrying,' said Tilly, miffed. 'I'm not used to all this exercise. I suppose that's why they picked me,' she added with a glum look. 'They thought I'd be just the person to hold you back.'

'Then I hope you'll be able to prove them wrong,' said Campbell, pausing on a ridge to look down at the river below.

His eyes scanned the valley. A television crew was waiting on the other side of the river, but there was no sign of the other contestants yet. They had taken the straightforward route, which meant that his gamble had paid off.

Tilly puffed up to stand beside him. 'Where next?'

Campbell pointed to the river. 'Down there.'

'But how...?' Tilly's heart sank as she peered over the edge at the precipitous drop.

'This is more like a cliff,' Campbell conceded.

'Oh, no...' Tilly started to back away as she realised just what he had in mind. 'No! No, absolutely not. There's no *way* I'm hanging off that rope again. Don't even think about it!'

CHAPTER TWO

TEN minutes later, Tilly was standing at the bottom, watching Campbell do his SAS act. Sliding down the cliff in one fluid action, he made it look so easy, she thought resentfully.

'There, that wasn't that bad, was it?' he said to her as he unclipped himself and began briskly coiling ropes.

'Yes, it was,' Tilly contradicted him sulkily, although it hadn't, in fact, been *quite* as bad as the first time. 'I'm going to be having nightmares about today for years,' she told him, unwilling to let him get away with his unashamed bullying that easily. 'I can't believe I was glad when I heard Greg wouldn't be able to take part! He would have been much nicer to me. I'm sure he would never have told me to stop being so wet or made me throw myself off the edge of a cliff,' she grumbled.

'I'm sure he'd have been perfect,' Campbell agreed. 'But he wouldn't have got you to the river ahead of everyone else.'

'He'd probably think there were more important things than winning,' said Tilly loftily.

Campbell looked at her as if she had suddenly started talking in Polish. Clearly it had never occurred to him that not coming first might occasionally be an option.

'Then why would he have been participating?'

'Perhaps he was the victim of emotional blackmail, like me.

This might come as news to you, but some of us think that it's enough to take part.'

'Tell that to the people hoping for a bed in the new hospice wing,' said Campbell brutally.

Tilly winced. He was right. She mustn't forget about why she was doing this, but if only there was some other way of raising money that didn't involve her being stuck in these freezing hills with the ultra-competitive Campbell Sanderson!

'Your company's sponsoring this whole show,' she said a little sulkily. 'Why don't you just hand out a few cheques instead of making everyone jump through all these hoops?'

'I couldn't agree with you more,' he said, to her surprise. She would have bet money on the fact that they would never agree about anything. 'I would much rather write cheques than spend a weekend messing around like this, but PR isn't my forte.'

'*No?*' said Tilly, feigning astonishment. 'You amaze me!'

Campbell shot her a look. 'Keith tells me programmes like this one are the way forward, viewers want to be engaged in the process of giving money, blah, blah, blah. The long and short of it is that I pay him a good salary as PR Director to know about these things and he assures me this is what will work best for Manning Securities.

'If it's the best thing for Manning, it's what I'm going to do,' he told her, 'and if I'm going to do it, I'm going to win it. In order for me to win, you've got to win, so you might as well get used to the idea. Any more questions?' he finished with one of his acerbic looks.

Tilly sighed and gave up. 'Did they say anything about lunch?'

For a moment Campbell stared at her, then the corner of his mouth quivered.

'No, but I imagine there'll be something to eat at the checkpoint across the river.'

Tilly looked away, thrown by the effect that quiver had had on her. For a moment there, he had looked quite human.

Quite attractive, too, her hormones insisted on pointing out, in spite of her best efforts to ignore them. That body combined with the undeniable *frisson* of a mysterious and possibly dangerous background was tempting enough, but if you threw in a glint of humour as well it made for a lethal combination.

She could do without finding Campbell Sanderson the slightest bit attractive. This whole weekend looked set to be humiliating enough without lusting after a man who would never in a million years lust back. That whole hard, couldn't-give-a-damn air gave him a kind of glamour, and Tilly was prepared to bet that there would be some lithe, beautiful, stylish woman lurking in the background.

Tilly could picture her easily, pouting when she heard that Campbell would be spending the entire weekend with another woman. *Don't go*, she would have said, tossing back her mane of silken hair and stretching her impossibly long, slender body invitingly. *Stay and make love to me instead.*

Of course it would take more than a sultry temptress to deflect Campbell's competitive spirit, but it would have been easy for him to reassure her. *There's no danger of me fancying the woman they've paired me with*, he would have said dismissively when she'd threatened to be jealous. *The television people have deliberately picked someone fat and dowdy to give the viewers a good laugh.*

Tilly could practically hear him saying it, and she scowled. No, she wouldn't be gratifying Seb and Harry by finding Campbell Sanderson attractive.

Well, not very attractive, anyway.

'Let's go, then,' she said. Campbell wasn't the only one who could do a good impression of don't-give-a-damn. 'I'm starving.'

She followed him down to the river's edge, where he walked up and down for a while, sussing out the situation while she eyed the river with some misgiving. It was wider than she had imagined, and the water was a deep, brackish brown and fast-flowing. It looked freezing.

If Campbell hadn't trailed the possibility of lunch on the other side, she would have been tempted to have given up there and then.

'Now what?' she asked as he prowled back. 'Surely they're not expecting us to throw up a pontoon bridge?'

She was joking, but Campbell seemed to think it was a serious suggestion. 'That'll take too long,' he said. 'Let's try further up.'

Still boggling at the idea that anyone would know how to build a pontoon bridge, let alone how long it would take, Tilly trotted after him.

'Where are you going?'

'To find a better crossing place.'

Perhaps lunch might not be such a distant possibility after all. Tilly brightened. 'Do you think there might be a bridge?'

'Not exactly,' said Campbell. He stopped abruptly as they skirted a bend and his eyes narrowed. 'Ah…that's more like it,' he said with satisfaction.

Tilly stared at the river. 'What is?'

'There,' he said. 'We can cross here.'

She stared harder. All she could see were a few boulders just peeking out of the rushing water. 'How?'

'Stepping stones,' he said. 'Couldn't be better.' He jumped lightly out on to the first boulder. 'We don't even need to get our feet wet.'

Leaping nimbly on to the next stone, he stopped and looked back to where Tilly was still standing on the bank. 'Aren't you coming? The sooner you get across, the sooner you get lunch.'

Did he think she couldn't work that out for herself?

'I'm *terribly* sorry.' She offered a sarcastic apology. 'Didn't they tell you I can't actually walk on water? I've been practising and practising, but I just can't get the hang of it somehow!'

'Look, it's just a step,' he said, impatience seeping into his voice once more.

'It's a step if you've got legs that are six feet long, which I haven't, in case you hadn't noticed.'

'OK, it's a jump, but you can do it easily.'

'I can't.'

'That's what you said about the abseil, and you did that.'

'Well, I really can't do this,' said Tilly crossly. 'I'll fall in.'

Muttering under his breath, Campbell stepped back on to the bank. 'Look, it's really not that far between each stone. Why don't I take your pack? You'll find it easier to balance without that.'

Tilly had to watch him stepping easily from stone to stone with an ease your average mountain goat would have envied before dumping both packs on the far bank and making his way back to her while she was still trying to formulate an excuse.

'Now it's your turn,' he said, waiting on the first boulder and stretching out a hand. 'All you need is a little jump and I'll pull you the rest of the way.'

'Oh, yes, I can see *that* working!' scoffed Tilly, with visions of her taking his hand and promptly pulling him into the water with her.

'Or shall I come and carry you across?'

'Don't even think about it!'

Out of the corner of her eye, she could see a cameraman approaching on the far bank. The crew had obviously spotted their approach from an unexpected angle and were hurrying to catch some entertaining moments on film. What a terrific shot it would make: Campbell trying to lift her, staggering under her weight, collapsing into the water with her. Ho, ho, ho. *How* everyone would laugh!

Over Tilly's dead body.

'All right,' she said quickly, seeing Campbell getting ready to come and fetch her if necessary. 'I'll jump.'

Without giving herself time to change her mind, she launched herself off the bank and Campbell only just managed to grab her and haul her on to the boulder with him. Tilly teetered wildly, only seconds from toppling backwards into the icy water before his arm clamped round her and pulled her hard against him.

He was steady as a rock and incredibly reassuring. Throwing pride to the chilly Scottish wind, Tilly clung to him.

'We must stop meeting like this,' he said dryly over the top of her head as she burrowed into him.

Aware of how ridiculous she must look but not daring to let go, Tilly did her best to play it cool. She kept her voice casual, as if she hadn't even noticed how strong and solid he was, or how good it felt to be held against a male body like his. Given that she was stranded in the middle of a freezing Scottish river, it was amazing that she was noticing anything about him at all.

'I usually like to get to know a man before I start hugging him,' she said, teeth chattering with a mixture of cold and nerves. 'You know, have a cup of coffee together or something first.'

'Our relationship does seem to have progressed quite quickly,' Campbell agreed over the top of her head. 'We'd hardly met before you were flinging your arms around my neck, and now this. I feel I should at least have sent you roses.'

There was a thread of amusement in his voice that only succeeded in flustering Tilly more.

'Roses will be the least I deserve if I survive today,' she said.

'Well, if we win, you can have a dozen,' said Campbell, looking for a way to get her to move on. Not that he wasn't appreciating having a soft feminine body squashed up against him, but the minutes were ticking by.

'Make that bars of chocolate and you're on,' said Tilly.

It would be too much to say that she was hot, stuck as she was on a rock in the middle of a freezing river with a chill wind whipping round her, but that was definitely warmth tingling in the pit of her stomach. This was one hell of a time for her hormones to start acting up.

'Do you think you're ready to try the next one then?'

She groaned a little. 'God, must I?'

'There's a camera trained on us right now,' Campbell pointed out. 'It must be getting a little boring for the cameraman, just the two of us entwined on a rock.'

If her hormones had their way it wouldn't be at all boring, Tilly thought. It could be extremely interesting, but knowing that a camera was pointing straight at her rather took the edge off any piquant little fantasies. Everyone knew that a camera added at least two sizes, and she didn't want to look any more ridiculous than she did already.

'OK, let's do it, then.'

Boulder by boulder, Campbell helped her across the river until there was just one last jump on to the bank. He went first and, the moment she let him go, Tilly started teetering. Her arms windmilled wildly and she took a wild leap for the bank before she fell back into the water.

Unprepared for her sudden jump, Campbell had no time to turn and catch her, and she missed her footing as she landed flat on her face, half on top of the bank, half down it. For a moment she lay stunned and splattered with mud before realising that she had provided the cameraman with his perfect action shot.

Excellent. She was *so* glad she was going to provide so much light entertainment for the viewers tucked up in their nice warm houses.

Tilly lifted her face from the mud. 'I want to go home,' she announced.

'You can't go home now. You're in the lead,' said Campbell, putting a hard hand under her arm and lifting her to her feet as easily as if she were a size six. It wasn't often that Tilly got to feel like thistledown, and she would have appreciated it more if she hadn't been spitting out mud. 'You're doing fine,' he told her.

'I am not doing fine. I'm making a prize prat of myself,' said Tilly bitterly, even as she bared her teeth in a smile for the camera which was zooming in on her.

'The viewers will love you,' soothed Campbell, helping her on with her backpack.

'Do you want to try that one again?' she enquired with a touch of acid. 'I think you'll find that the correct reply there was, *No, of course you're not making a prat of yourself, Tilly.*'

The corner of his mouth quirked. 'Would you believe me if I said that now?'

'Obviously not,' said Tilly crisply as she tried to quell her fickle senses, which were fizzing at the mere hint of a proper smile.

'Then I'll save my breath. Come on, we're nearly at the end of the first section. You'll feel better when you've had some lunch.'

Lunch wasn't very exciting, but at least it was provided. As she plodded after Campbell to the checkpoint, a horrible thought occurred to Tilly. What if they were expected to take survival skills to the extreme? She wouldn't put it past the television crew to make them catch their own rabbit or dig up worms for a quick snack.

In the event, the flaccid cheese and tomato sandwiches were a huge relief and Tilly devoured all of hers before Campbell, who had been in discussion with the producer, came over.

'What happens now?' she asked, her heart sinking at the sight of the map under his arm.

'We were first across, so we're definitely through to the next round.'

'Fabulous.' Tilly sighed.

Why couldn't she have been paired with a loser? He would have been much more her style, after all, and she could have been waiting for the bus home right now, which would have suited her fine.

Then she remembered the hospice, and what it had meant to her mother, to all of them, and immediately felt guilty. She shouldn't be wishing they could lose just so she could go home and get warm and comfortable.

'What do we have to do now?' she asked Campbell to make up for it.

'We have to get ourselves to the top of Ben Nuarrh.'

'Where's that?' Already Tilly knew that she wasn't going to like the answer.

It was even worse than she had feared. Campbell squinted into the distance and pointed at a jagged hill just visible in the purplish grey haze on the horizon. 'That's Ben Nuarrh.'

'But that's *miles*!' she said, aghast.

'It's a fair trek,' he agreed.

'We'll never do that this afternoon!'

'No, we'll have to camp. They've given us a tent and supplies.'

'A *tent*?' This was getting worse and worse. 'Nobody said anything to me about camping!'

'You must have been told you'd be away all weekend, weren't you?'

'Well, yes, but I thought we'd be staying in some lovely hotel. A baronial hall or something, with antlers in the library and a fire and deep baths and clean sheets...' Tilly trailed off. 'I should have known.' She sighed. 'My fantasies never turn into reality.'

Campbell lifted an eyebrow. 'What, never?'

Well, there had been Olivier. He had been a dream come true, at least at first, Tilly remembered, but the rest of her fantasy hadn't come to anything, had it? It had been so lovely, too. Olivier would look at her one day and the scales would fall from his eyes. *You're beautiful, Tilly*, he would say. *Marry me and share my life for ever.*

No, that fantasy hadn't lasted, she thought a little sadly. Not that there was any need to tell Campbell Sanderson that. A girl had to have some pride.

She lifted her chin. 'Hardly ever,' she said.

'Maybe you need to have more realistic fantasies,' he said.

'Like what?'

'Like a tent that doesn't leak, or a dry sleeping bag…or a bar of chocolate to have halfway there.'

Tilly was unimpressed. 'The chocolate sounds OK,' she conceded, 'but otherwise that's not really the stuff my fantasies are made of.'

'What about the fantasy of winning this challenge?'

'That's your fantasy, not mine,' Tilly objected, but she got to her feet, brushing the crumbs from her lap. 'Still, may as well try and make your fantasy come true at least.'

'That's not an offer a man gets every day.'

His mouth was doing that infuriating, tantalizing half-smile again. Tilly averted her gaze firmly and tried not to think about what other fantasies he might have that would be a lot more fun to help him with than traipsing up and down bloody mountains.

However, winning seemed to be all Campbell was interested in right then. 'We've got a good forty-five minutes on the others,' he told her with satisfaction as they went to collect the extra equipment. 'We'll be well ahead by the end of the day.'

He put the tent and most of the food in his own rucksack, deftly packing everything away.

'I'll take the chocolate,' Tilly offered generously, but Campbell only sent her an ironic glance.

'I think I'd better keep it,' he said. 'I may need it to get you up that mountain.'

'It'll take more than chocolate.' She sighed, thinking of the long afternoon ahead of her.

'It's a challenge,' he reminded her, handing her the lighter rucksack.

'I've been challenged enough today,' she grumbled, but she put the pack on. 'I've abseiled—twice!—and forded a river, and walked for *miles*… It's only lunchtime and I'm exhausted! I don't need any more challenges.'

Campbell tsk-tsked. 'That's not the right attitude, Jenkins. You're supposed to be thinking positive.'

'Don't call me Jenkins,' said Tilly crossly as she jerked the straps into place. 'It makes me feel as if I should be doing press ups and shouting *sir!*'

Ignoring her, Campbell turned to the producer, Suzy, who had come over to give them their final instructions before they set off.

'You know where you're going, and where the final checkpoint is?' she asked.

'All under control,' Campbell told her.

'Have you got everything you need?'

'A lift home would be nice,' muttered Tilly before Campbell frowned her down.

'We're fine.'

'Roger and Leanne were second across, so they'll be racing you to the top and back,' said Suzy. 'Roger's got GPS,' she added. 'That'll give them an advantage, but we've got it here, and I can give it to you, too, if you like.'

'What's GPS?' asked Tilly.

'It's a satellite navigation gizmo,' said Campbell dismissively. 'Some people can't get from A to B without them.'

'Is that what Roger had on his watch?'

Tilly remembered Roger showing Leanne his watch and explaining loudly how it would not only tell him where he was but could measure altitude, barometric pressure, temperature and even his heart rate.

It wasn't just his watch that was top of the range either. Roger's jacket was apparently a wonder of technology, his boots were cutting edge and his thermal underwear had been tested under polar conditions. He had the gear for every eventuality.

Next to Roger, Campbell had cut an unimpressive figure. He had no fancy watch, no smart jacket, not even a plastic cover to stop his map getting wet. His trousers were tucked into thick socks and old leather boots, and he wore a thick blue Guernsey—oh, and a contemptuous expression, although Tilly couldn't see why he was sneering at Roger. Roger was younger than Campbell and much better looking.

He smiled a lot, too, unlike some people who couldn't manage much more than a twitch at the corner of their mouths, she remembered with a darkling glance at Campbell.

If GPS told you where you were, it sounded a very good thing to Tilly. 'I think we should take one, just in case,' she said, but was overruled by Campbell.

'We've got a map,' he said with finality. 'That's all we need.'

'I'm surprised you're even deigning to take a map,' Tilly grumbled. 'I'd got you down as one of those men who refuses to even look at a map. I bet you think you can get wherever you're going by some kind of primeval instinct, as if you've got some universal A to Z encoded in your genes. I'm right, aren't I? How many times have you driven round and round for *hours* rather than give in to the woman sitting beside you who's bleating, "Why don't we stop and ask for directions?"'

Campbell opened his mouth to make a cutting reply, but Suzy

got in first. 'That's great!' she said enthusiastically. 'There's real chemistry between you two. The viewers will love it!'

'What viewers?' said Tilly blankly.

'This is a television programme,' Suzy reminded her. 'That's why we've been filming you.'

'What, just now?' Tilly cast a hunted look around. Sure enough, one of the cameramen was filming them from a few feet away. 'I thought it would be just when we were doing stuff,' she whispered, hurriedly turning her back on him.

'The interaction between you is just as interesting as how you get down a cliff or across a river,' Suzy explained patiently. 'The winners won't necessarily be the ones who get to the end first. They'll be the ones the viewers vote for, the ones they like and feel they can identify with. That reminds me,' she said and dug in her bag. 'You'll need this.'

She produced a smart little video camera and handed it to Campbell.

'What's this for?'

'You'll have to film yourselves at the top of Ben Nuarrh, and then of course you'll have to keep a video diary.'

'*What?*' Campbell's brows snapped together and Tilly stared, united for once in their consternation.

'The viewers aren't just interested in whether you can rise to these challenges or not,' said Suzy. 'They want to know your reactions, too. Video diaries are a great way to get insight into what people really feel, and of course they're very visual, too. People tend to treat them like a confessional. There's nobody asking questions. It's just you talking to the camera on your own, and it's much harder to pretend somehow when you're alone. People say things they wouldn't dream of admitting in front of anyone else.'

Campbell was appalled at the very idea. He had got through life perfectly well without ever talking about his feelings and he had no intention of starting now. They could whistle if they wanted anything interesting out of him!

'We don't both have to do them, surely?'

'Of course you do.' Suzy was firm. 'We're interested in how you react to each other. For this part of the challenge, you're the one who knows what he's doing, but for the next part, it'll be Tilly who's in charge.'

'What next part?' asked Campbell with foreboding.

'When Tilly teaches you how to make and decorate a wedding cake.' Suzy's smile faltered as she saw his expression. 'Didn't Keith tell you?'

'No.' His voice was grim. 'He omitted that part.'

No doubt because Keith had known exactly how Campbell would react! He'd thought it would just be a question of getting Tilly to the last checkpoint before anyone else. Physical challenges, he could deal with. A race was no problem, but making a *cake*? What a ridiculous waste of time!

'I'm not sure I can do that,' he said.

'Oh, come now,' said Tilly, who had been watching his expression and reading it without any difficulty. 'That's not the right attitude, Sanderson,' she quoted his words back at him wickedly. 'You're supposed to be thinking positive.'

The look he shot her promised vengeance but, with the camera still trained on them, he had to refrain from the murder that was clearly on his mind.

Tilly didn't care. This was the first time she had enjoyed herself all day. Let Campbell Sanderson see what it was like to be made to do something completely alien! Suddenly she could see the point of the programme. She would be able to get her own back when he was in her kitchen. All she had to do was survive Ben Nuarrh.

'I'm thinking about *timing*.' Campbell frowned at her before turning to Suzy to explain. 'I'm leaving Manning very soon and moving to a new job in the States. Obviously, I've got a lot to do before then.'

Suzy was dismayed. 'If you can't do the second part of the challenge, we'll have to cut you,' she said. 'That would be such a shame! We've got some great footage of you two already. Roger and Leanne are doing well, too. If you drop out, it'll probably mean a walkover for them, and then the competition would lose any tension. You know, it could be worse than a wedding cake,' she added in a wheedling voice. 'Roger's got to learn to do a pedicure.'

'Plus, they'll all think we dropped out because we were losing,' said Tilly, knowing Campbell would hate the very thought. It wasn't that she cared about winning, but she wanted her revenge for today's humiliations.

Campbell sucked in an irritable breath. He had a fairly clear idea of why Tilly was so keen for them to continue. She might look sweet with that rosy, heart-shaped face but there was an intriguing tartness to her, too. She would no doubt be hoping that it would be his turn to make a fool of himself next.

Let her hope. Campbell had no intention of indulging her. If he pulled out now, there would be no question of winning and, having got this far, he was loath to give up. How hard could it be to make a cake, after all? It wouldn't take long, and if he needed to make more time, he would just delegate a few things to Keith. Serve him right for getting him into this mess in the first place.

'But if we're carrying on with the competition, we're going to win,' he warned Tilly as they said goodbye to Suzy and set off towards Pen Nuarrh. 'That means no more dawdling!'

He set a punishing pace and Tilly was soon struggling. 'Can't we stop for five minutes so I can get my breath back?' she pleaded at last.

'You can have a rest when we get to the top.'

When she finally clambered up to where Campbell was waiting, Tilly was wheezing and bright red in the face.

'God, this is killing me!' She collapsed on to a rock while she struggled for breath. 'If this is just a hill, I'm never going to get to the top of that mountain.'

'You're very unfit,' he said disapprovingly.

Tilly scowled. 'Why not come right out and say I'm fat?'

'I would if that's what I thought,' he retorted. 'You're screwed up about your weight, clearly, but you don't look fat to me. You *do* seem unfit. Don't you take any exercise?'

'Not if I can help it,' said Tilly, only slightly mollified. 'I'm too busy.'

'Making cakes?' Campbell didn't bother to hide his disbelief.

'Yes, making cakes,' she said evenly. She was used to men pooh-poohing what she did for a living. 'It's my business.'

Campbell unscrewed a water bottle and passed it over to her. 'Doesn't that get boring?'

She shook her head as she drank gratefully. 'I love it. And every cake I make is different. It's not just piping endless icing roses for traditional wedding cakes. Every one I make is unique. I spend a lot of time talking to my clients so that I can come up with an individual design for their special occasion.'

'Like what?'

'It was some guy's fortieth birthday the other day, and he'd always dreamt of having a Porsche. His wife couldn't afford one of those, obviously, but she got me to make a cake in the shape of a Porsche 911, down to the last detail. Or I quite often make shoes or bags for girls' twenty-first birthdays—they're always fun.'

Campbell's eyes rested on her face. She was recovering from her breathlessness and her colour was fading, but she still glowed pinkly. Her eyes were a dark and rather beautiful blue, he found himself noticing, and the lush mouth curved in re-membered enthusiasm.

He wished he hadn't noticed quite how warm and soft and inviting it looked.

He looked away.

'I've never thought of cakes as fun before,' he said.

'I've never thought of climbing hills as fun either,' said Tilly frankly. She blew out a breath and pushed her hair back from her face. 'I suppose they put us together because we're so incompatible.'

'That was the general idea,' said Campbell.

'I wonder if Roger and Leanne found anything in common?'

Campbell snorted. 'Roger could always use his GPS. He says he can find anything with that.'

They glanced at each other, then suddenly both began to laugh, although Tilly was so startled by the effect a smile had on Campbell's expression that she almost stopped. Who would have thought a laugh could make such a difference? A mere crease of the cheeks, a simple curve of the mouth, a brief glimpse of strong white teeth? That was all it was, really.

The cool green eyes were lit with amusement as they met hers, and Tilly felt her heart give an odd little skip that left her almost breathless. It was as if a switch had been flipped, brightening the light so that she could see him in extraordinary detail—the pores of his skin, the dark ring around his pale irises, every hair in the thick brows—and she was abruptly aware of him as a powerful male animal, all muscle and leashed strength.

The image made Tilly blink and sent heat flooding through her, reaching places that hadn't tingled in quite that way for a very long time. Jerking her gaze away from his, she took a long glug from the water bottle, aware that her cheeks were burning.

Well, she would be hot, wouldn't she? She had just climbed a huge hill.

CHAPTER THREE

SHE hoped that was the reason, anyway.

There wasn't much point in finding man like Campbell Sanderson attractive, she reminded herself glumly. He was out of her league.

Friends would be furious if they knew she was thinking like that. Cleo was always urging her to forget Olivier and boost her ego with a quick fling. 'You need to feel good about yourself again,' she would insist to Tilly. 'You don't need to fall in love again just yet. You just need some fun. Find someone attractive and have a good time for a while. Think of it as a transitional relationship.'

The idea sounded good in principle but, as Tilly had discovered, it was a lot harder to put into practice. Even if her confidence had been up to it, attractive single men were in short supply in Allerby.

Anyway, Campbell wouldn't be single, she decided. He must be in his late thirties, and even SAS types surely fell prey to a committed relationship of some kind somewhere along the line. He had probably been snapped up by someone slender and beautiful and—even worse—really nice long ago.

There was no sign of a wedding ring, of course, but macho men like him wouldn't wear anything that remotely smacked of jewellery. So he *might* be married.

Or he might not.

Studying him covertly, Tilly drank some more water and wondered if she could ask him outright. It might seem a bit obvious, especially when they were going to be sleeping together in a tiny tent.

Sleeping together. Hmm. What was *that* going to be like?

Cleo would have told her to make the most of the opportunity but, like all of Cleo's ideas, that was easier said than done. Tilly only had to look at Campbell to know that *he* certainly wasn't fizzing with anticipation at the thought of sleeping close to her. He probably hadn't given the issue of sleeping arrangements a moment's thought.

He wouldn't care *what* happened as long as he won this stupid race.

Tilly sighed inwardly. That was just her luck. She had finally stumbled across an attractive man only to discover that, even given the remote off-chance that he might be available, he was far too competitive to let himself be distracted by the possibilities of a man and a woman in a small tent.

Look at him now—totally focused, glancing at his watch, determined to keep her moving.

'Let's get going,' he said.

Tilly groaned but hauled herself obediently to her feet. 'How much further is it?'

'We could do another three hours at least.'

'I'm not sure my feet will last that long,' she said, wincing as she wriggled her toes in her boots.

'Mind over matter,' said Campbell briskly. He threw his pack on to his back and adjusted the straps with deft movements. 'The trick is to keep thinking about something else.'

'Like what?'

'Like what you'd really like to find at the top of the next hill.'

'That's easy,' said Tilly, securing her own pack into place and trudging after him. 'Can you please make sure there's a fabulous bathroom, with a deep, scented bath piled high with bubbles? I'd like candles and a glass of champagne waiting for me on the edge of the bath…oh, and a little plate of nibbles, too. Smoked salmon, probably,' she added reflectively. 'Or nuts? No, smoked salmon,' she decided. 'Little roulades stuffed with prawn mousse and soft cheese.'

'I'll see what I can do,' said Campbell in a dry voice.

He was taken aback by how vividly he could picture Tilly sinking into the water with a sigh of pleasure. Her skin would be pink and pearly and wet, her hair clinging in damp tendrils around her face, her breasts rising out of the bubbles as she tipped back her head and dropped smoked salmon into that lush mouth…

Campbell had to give himself a mental shake, and he picked up his stride. He felt almost embarrassed, as if someone had caught him peeking round the bathroom door.

Tilly was still fantasising. 'While you're at it, can you arrange for a wonderful meal to be cooking so that the smell comes wafting up the stairs? No niminy piminy nouvelle cuisine, though, not after the day I've had. I want something hot and tasty. It doesn't have to be fancy.'

'A roast?' Campbell suggested, drawn back into the scene she was creating in spite of himself.

'Yes, a roast would be very acceptable, especially if you can lay on all the trimmings, too. Or a really good casserole with creamy mashed potatoes.' Tilly was beginning to salivate now. She could practically taste that first mouthful. 'Or—I know!— steak and kidney pudding…mmm, yum, yum… Even a—'

Glancing at Campbell just then and catching his fascinated gaze, she broke off. 'What—you don't have fantasies?'

'Not about food.'

'What *do* you fantasise about then?' she demanded grouchily, embarrassed at having revealed quite how greedy she was. Why couldn't she be the kind of girl who hankered after a green salad or a mug of nice herbal tea?

Campbell lifted an eyebrow in response, and she tutted. 'Not *that* kind of fantasy,' she scolded as if he had spoken, although actually she wouldn't have minded knowing that at all. 'A fantasy you can share with a nice girl like me!'

'I'm not sure any of my fantasies are suitable for nice girls.'

There was just the faintest thread of amusement in his voice and Tilly was sure that he was mocking her.

'All right, imagine being really relaxed,' she challenged him.

'What?'

'Just do it,' she insisted. 'Close your eyes—or, on second thoughts, you'd better not, you might trip—and picture yourself happy.'

Campbell sighed and prepared to indulge her. At least it might stop her whingeing about her feet for a while longer. He thought for a moment.

'OK.'

'Have you an image of yourself relaxed and happy?'

'Yes.'

'Where are you?'

Tilly hoped that he wasn't going to say that he was in bed. That would make it very hard to concentrate. She waited for him to say *standing on top of a mountain* or *skiing down a black run*.

'I'm sitting in a comfortable chair in front of the fire.'

It was so unexpected that she actually gaped at him. *Sitting?* Wasn't that a bit tame for a man like Campbell?

'What are you doing?'

'Reading.'

The defensive note in his voice made Tilly grin. 'You make it sound like you're confessing a dirty secret! What are you reading? Nothing illegal or immoral, I hope.'

'Roman military history.'

Campbell practically bit out the words, and this time Tilly really did laugh.

He scowled at her. 'What's so funny?'

'I'm sorry. It was just so unexpected,' she tried to explain.

'What, marines aren't allowed to read?'

'It's not that. It's just that you seem such a macho action man that it's hard to imagine you poring over ancient history, that's all.'

'I don't want to spend all day doing it. You asked me to imagine myself relaxed,' said Campbell almost crossly. 'That was just a picture that came into my mind. Obviously I should have said some kind of extreme sport instead!'

'That wouldn't have been as interesting, though,' said Tilly, meaning it, but Campbell clearly thought that she was joking.

'I've had the mick taken out of me for years,' he said in a resigned voice. 'Anyone would think I had some bizarre fetish. It's only military history, for God's sake.'

'But why the Romans?'

He shrugged. 'I like their logical approach. Their sense of order. They were great engineers. Great strategists.'

'And successful,' Tilly reminded him, sure that was the key to their appeal for him. 'The Romans were winners, too.' She caught his look. 'Hey, I did history at school. Roman history may not be my bedtime reading, but I'm not completely ignorant!'

She studied him from under her lashes as she toiled on beside him. She hoped he wasn't regretting telling her. She rather liked the idea of him sitting quietly and reading by the fire, and was touched by the fact that he seemed faintly embarrassed by it, as if he had confessed some weakness.

'So…have you got a fantasy meal cooking in the background while you read your book?'

'I'm afraid I'm not someone who spends a lot of time

thinking about food,' he said. 'I eat what's put in front of me. I'll have some of your roast.'

Tilly wished he hadn't said that. It was enough to conjure up an instant cosy domestic scene. There she was, upstairs in the bath, and there was Campbell by the fire. Any minute now he would look at his watch, put his book down and go and check on the roast, then he would come upstairs and sit on the edge of the bath.

I've turned the potatoes, he would say, topping up her glass. If you were going to have a fantasy, Tilly believed, you might as well make it a really good one. *Will you be much longer?*

And Tilly would sip her champagne and ask him to wash her back while he was there. She could almost feel his warm, firm hands soaping her, and obviously he wouldn't stop at her back...

'That must be some bath.'

Campbell's voice jerked Tilly out of her daydream. 'What?' Disorientated, she looked around her to find that she had somehow made it to the top of the hill without even realising it.

'You haven't said a word for the last mile. I'm impressed by the power of your fantasising!'

If only he knew.

A guilty flush stained Tilly's cheeks and her eyes slid away from his just in case an ability to mind-read was something else he had forgotten to mention, along with a knowledge of ancient military history.

Now that she had snapped out of it, she was appalled at herself. What had she been *thinking*? Harry and Seb had been right. She had been on her own too long. It was time she found another man.

At least she knew she was over Olivier. He had been the focus of her fantasies for quite a while, most of them involving him crawling back and confessing that he had made a terrible mistake. Satisfying in their own way, but nowhere near as erotic as the one that had carried her up the hillside.

'Perhaps I can make one of your fantasies come true,' said Campbell, digging in his rucksack.

For a blanket? Tilly wondered wildly and gulped. She must get a grip.

'Which one?' she asked, appalled to hear that her voice came out as barely more than a croak.

'Chocolate,' he said, and produced a bar. 'You can have a rest for ten minutes, too.'

Tilly didn't know whether she was disappointed or relieved. 'Great,' she said weakly.

The light was already going from the sky and the air was cooling rapidly as she perched on her pack. Unwrapping the chocolate, she broke the bar in half and offered part to Campbell, who shook his head.

'You have it,' he said.

He was fast becoming a fantasy man in reality, thought Tilly ruefully. A man who gave you chocolate and insisted you ate it all without sharing.

Unaware of the trend of her thoughts, Campbell was unfolding the map that he had shoved carelessly into his pocket.

'Isn't it a bit late to be looking at that now?' said Tilly through a mouthful of chocolate. 'I hope you're not about to tell me that we've climbed the wrong hills?'

She almost wished he would so that she could go back to feeling cross with him. It would be a lot easier than this unnerving awareness. See what happened when you let your fantasies get out of control?

'No, we're in the right place. I'm sure Roger's GPS would tell us exactly the same thing.'

'Then why aren't they here with us?'

'We had a head start, remember? And Roger may well take a different route to Ben Nuarrh.'

'I bet it's an easier one!'

'This is quicker,' said Campbell firmly.

He passed Tilly the map. 'We're here,' he said, pointing, and Tilly found her eyes riveted on his hand. The one that had done such incredible things with the soap in her fantasy...

'Concentrate, Jenkins!' Campbell's peremptory tone made her jump. 'You're fading out, there.'

'Oh...um, yes...sorry...I'm just a bit tired.'

A frown touched his eyes as he glanced at her. 'I thought we'd camp there,' he said, moving his finger on the map. 'Do you think you can make it, or will you need a new fantasy to get you there?'

Tilly swallowed. 'I think I've done enough fantasising for today!'

'Are you ready to get on, then? I can't promise a bath or a bed, but we'll have something to eat and you'll be able to sleep.'

'That'll be enough for me,' said Tilly.

It was a mistake to have stopped. She found the last leg a real struggle. The threatened blister had become a reality, and her feet were killing her. She was stiff, too, and tired and cold.

Seeing her hobbling, Campbell took her pack for her and managed to walk just as easily with two. He stayed beside her, encouraging her up the last steep slope, and refusing to let her stop when she threatened to collapse.

Tilly couldn't have done it without him, but she was vaguely distrustful of his motives all the same. It was all very well being Mr Nice Guy *now*. She might appreciate his help, but she knew quite well that he was only doing it because he wanted to get to the top of Ben Nuarrh first.

Her father was just the same—determined to get his own way whatever happened. If charm was the easiest way to get what he wanted, he would lay it on with a trowel, but he would never lose sight of his goal. Tilly had learnt early to distrust men who'd do anything to win, but it was still hard not to warm treacherously at the approval in Campbell's voice as he practically carried her the last few yards.

'Well done.'

It was almost dark by then, so Tilly couldn't see much. They were somewhere high on the flank of Ben Nuarrh, that much she knew, and Campbell seemed to have found a sheltered hollow where a peaty burn ran between granite outcrops and there was enough flattish, if somewhat soggy, ground to set up the tent.

He lowered her on to one of the outcrops and she sat, numb with exhaustion, and watched as he put up the tent with an efficiency that didn't surprise her in the least. Unrolling the bedding, he backed out and held open the flap.

'Why don't you get in?' he said to Tilly. 'You can take off your boots and do your video diary while I make the stew.'

'Stew?' She gaped at him, wondering how on earth he was going to conjure a casserole out of his pack.

'Don't get excited. It's a dehydrated pack—add to boiling water and stir, which is pretty much my level of cooking. It won't be your fantasy, but it'll be hot and filling.'

'I suppose that's better than nothing,' she said, getting up stiffly and hobbling to the tent.

It was very small. She bent and peered inside. 'Is there going to be room for both of us?' she asked doubtfully.

'It'll be tight, but that's a good thing. We won't be wasting body warmth,' said Campbell. 'But don't worry,' he added ironically as she straightened. 'We've separate sleeping bags.'

Tilly wasn't sure how to respond to that. She couldn't decide whether to make it clear that she was relieved, or play it cool, as if she took the prospect of sharing sleeping bags in her stride the whole time.

Or perhaps this was a good opportunity to find out a bit more about him?

'Still, it's going to be very cosy,' she said. 'Are you going to have some explaining to do when you get down?'

'What do you mean?' Campbell glanced up from where he was setting up a portable gas ring with his usual deftness and economy of movement.

'Well, if I discovered that my husband or boyfriend had spent the night with another woman in a tent this size I wouldn't be very happy about it.'

'Oh, I see,' he said, returning his attention to the gas. 'No, there's no one I need to explain anything to, and that's the way I like it.'

'You're not married then?'

'Not any more.'

'I'm sorry.' Tilly hesitated by the tent entrance. 'What happened?'

Campbell sighed and sat back on his heels, looking up at her with a sardonic expression. 'Does it matter?'

'God, you can tell you're a man who's been trained to withstand interrogation,' grumbled Tilly. Talk about trying to get blood out of a stone! 'Don't they teach you the art of conversation in the Marines? I just thought it would be nice to find out a bit more about the man I'm going to be sleeping with,' she told him with a huffy look and then, to her fury, blushed when he lifted one amused brow at her choice of words. 'In a manner of speaking,' she added stiffly.

'Lisa left me for another man who could give her more than I could. We got divorced. She's married again and lives in the States now. End of story.'

'Do you have any kids?'

'Nope.'

Tilly sighed. 'I was about to say that must make it easier because that's what people always say when a relationship breaks down. *At least there weren't any children.* As if it helps somehow,' she remembered with a bitter edge to her voice. 'When someone leaves you, it doesn't hurt any less just because you haven't got children.'

'Sounds like you're speaking from experience,' Campbell commented.

'I am.'

'Well, you don't need to feel sorry for me,' he told her, ignoring the opportunity to say that he felt sorry for *her*, Tilly couldn't help noting. 'It was a disaster from the start. I should never have married her.'

'Then why did you?'

He shrugged. 'Why? Because Lisa was—is—the most beautiful woman I've ever seen. She's absolutely dazzling. The moment I saw her, I had to have her.'

Tilly tried—and failed—to imagine a man ever saying that about her.

'You must have loved her.'

'Are you going to take your boots off?' Campbell made it plain the conversation was over by getting to his feet.

Clearly *not* a man who believed in talking things through.

Resigned to the fact that she wasn't going to get any more out of him, Tilly applied herself to the problem of actually getting into the tent. She was so tired that she was afraid that once she was in she would never get out again. Campbell had managed to make it look a perfectly simple business—he would—but she was reduced to kneeling down and then attempting an undignified dive inside between the entrance flaps.

Once in, she had to wriggle around until she was in a

position where she could sit up and take off her boots—no easy task in itself. Campbell had set up a light near the entrance, which she had managed to knock over twice during her ungainly entrance, but at least it meant she could see what she was doing.

Pulling off the second boot with a gusty sigh of relief, Tilly collapsed back on to her sleeping bag and stared up at the weird shadows the light cast on the orange roof of the tent. She couldn't remember ever being so tired, or so cold.

'I don't think I'll ever be able to move again,' she shouted out to Campbell, who had been to the nearby stream and boiled some water in the time it had taken her to sort herself out. 'I'm going to have to spend the rest of my life here. They'll find me in five thousand years, frozen like that prehistoric hunter guy in a glacier, and use my body to find out about twenty-first century society.'

Tilly rather liked the idea of scientists of the future poring over her body and speculating about her life. 'They'll decide I lived and worked up here, and that red salopettes were the height of fashion.'

Outside the tent, she could see Campbell shaking his head in disbelief. 'You have the most extraordinary imagination,' he said.

'All that research,' said Tilly, too carried away by her idea to care what he thought, 'and none of them will know that I was only stuck up here because my loathsome brothers thought I should get out of my rut!

'This is all their fault,' she went on bitterly. 'They'll be sorry when I'm not there to cook for them and show them how to use the washing machine and be nice to their girlfriends! *If only we hadn't been so stupid*, they'll say to each other. *What were we thinking? Dear Tilly could still be with us instead of stuck up on that mountain.*'

'Dear Tilly will be back with them by tomorrow night,' said Campbell, unmoved by her story. 'I'm not going to leave you here.'

'You would if you thought you could win without me,' said Tilly sulkily.

'Fortunately for you, I can't.'

Ducking into the tent, he handed her an enamel mug of black tea. 'Have this to warm you up while I get the stew going.'

'Warm? Warm? What's warm?' She shivered but took the tea gratefully. 'The only trouble with stopping is realising how cold you are.'

Campbell tsk-tsked. 'Stop complaining,' he said 'Have one of your fantasies instead—or, better still, do the video diary.' He dug around in his rucksack for the camera.

'Why do I have to do it?' grumbled Tilly as he held it to the light so that he could see how it worked.'

'Because you'll be better at that than me.'

'I won't. I'd feel a complete idiot talking to a camera,' she protested. 'I wouldn't know what to say.'

'Just carry on wittering the way you've been doing all day,' suggested Campbell with a touch of acid. 'Tell them one of your fantasies—that should win a few votes!'

'I'm not going to do that!' She flopped back down on to the sleeping bag. 'Why don't we pretend we forgot about the video diary business?'

He shook his head firmly. 'We can't do that. The diary is part of the challenge.' Propping the camera on top of his rucksack, he bent down to peer through it and check that it was pointing at Tilly. 'You heard what Suzy said. We're going to be judged on the video diary and film clips as well as on who gets back down from Ben Nuarrh first.'

'If you care so much about winning, you do it,' said Tilly crossly.

'I've got to make the stew.' Campbell moved the lamp so that the light fell on her. 'Look, just talk for a minute and then it's done. You don't even have to get up. I promise I won't listen, so you can be as horrible about me as you want.'

He pointed at a button on top of the camera. 'I'll set it going. Just press this when you've finished.'

'Hang on!' Tilly started to struggle up in protest, but he was already crawling out of the tent, leaving the red light beckoning encouragingly.

Tilly's video diary:
[Staring at camera with a hunted look] Oh, God, I suppose I'll have to say something… Um… [Long pause] OK, here I am, halfway up a Scottish mountain with a man I'd never met before this morning. It's funny to think that this time last night I'd never even heard of Campbell, and now it seems as if I've known him for ever. And tonight we're going to sleep together…well, not sleep together, except of course we will *be sleeping…oh, you know what I mean. Can whoever's watching this edit that bit out? [Yawns hugely] I'm so tired, I can't think straight!*

Where was I? Oh, yes, Campbell… Well, he was a terrible bully this morning. You should have seen him making me abseil down that cliff—two cliffs! Talk about competitive! And he's not exactly chatty. I've never met a man who talks so little about himself, to be honest. His middle name must be Clam. Campbell the Clam Sanderson. [Giggles]

At least they'd never have to worry about him blabbing operational secrets. I bet he was in one of those special units, you know. No point in asking him, though. He'd just say he could tell me, but he'd have to kill me. He probably would, too. Still, I'm sure Suzy's assistant is right. He's got that steely-eyed thing going that's quite exciting when

he's not pushing you down a cliff [Pauses, looks doubtful]
Actually, could you cut that bit, too?

[Yawns again, belatedly covering mouth] Anyway, he
wasn't so bad this afternoon. In fact, he was really quite
nice, especially the last few miles. [Pauses again, re-
membering] Yes, surprisingly nice. And now he's making
me supper. I'm not sure what this stew is going to be like,
though. Dehydrated doesn't sound very nice, but I'm so
hungry I'll eat it. I ought to offer to help, but I really don't
think I've got the energy to get out of the tent. [Slides out
of view of camera] Perhaps if I just closed my eyes for a
moment, and then I'll go and give him a hand...

Campbell looked up from the pot he was stirring, suddenly
alert. He could hear the wind whistling around the crags, the
canvas flapping, the hiss of the gas, but when he listened, he
realised there was something missing.

No Tilly. How long was it since he had heard her voice?
'Tilly?'

He bent down to peer into the tent. She had crashed out over both
sleeping bags, and appeared to have simply toppled from where
she had been sitting talking to the camera and was sound asleep.

Shaking his head, Campbell turned off the camera.

Tilly was still fully dressed apart from her boots, and he con-
templated her slumped form with a slight frown. How was he
going to get her into her sleeping bag? He had no intention of
undressing her, but she would be better off without her jacket.
Its stiff fabric was digging into her face as it was. It would certainly be uncomfortable if she did wake up and, besides, she
would need the jacket as an extra layer to put on in the morning.

'Tilly?' he tried again, but she was dead to the world and
didn't even stir when he lifted her up to pull her arms out of
the sleeves and get rid of the jacket.

It was like dealing with a very large floppy doll, although he imagined dolls weren't usually that warm and soft. Not having had even a sister, Campbell's experience of dolls was negligible, but he was fairly sure they didn't smell faintly of…what was it? He sniffed. Some flower. Roses, perhaps? He had never been very good on flowers but something about the fragrance of Tilly's hair reminded him of his mother's garden on a summer evening long ago.

The thought made Campbell frown. He wasn't supposed to be thinking about things like that. Unzipping one of the sleeping bags, he manoeuvred Tilly inside it, not without difficulty. Quite a bit of manhandling was required and he was very aware of her lush body even through the layers of clothing. It was all very well staying focused but it was hard not to be distracted by the fact that, whatever else Tilly might be, she was all woman.

An exasperating one, Campbell reminded himself. At least she was quiet now that she was sleeping. He had never met anyone quite so chatty. Lisa had been mistress of icy silence, and he wasn't at all sure which was worse.

Tilly stirred and mumbled something as he tucked her legs into the sleeping bag and zipped her up. The next moment she was turning and snuggling down like a child with more unintelligible mumbling and some smacking of her lips before she sank back into a deep sleep.

Campbell sat back on his heels and watched her for a moment. It was the first chance he had had to look at her properly, he realised, and without that challenging blue gaze fixed on him he could see that she had lovely creamy skin and beautiful eyebrows. The heart-shaped face was slack with sleep, but her generous mouth still had a humorous curve to it, as if she were on the point of smiling.

Even now, sound asleep, there was something *disorderly*

about her, Campbell decided. She was all softness and curves and curls, and it made him twitchy. There were no straight lines with Tilly, no logic, no control. She talked the whole time and her imagination was so vivid he wasn't sure whether she was talking nonsense or not half the time.

His eyes rested on her mouth almost unwillingly. Tilly might be high-maintenance, but there was a warmth and a sweetness about her, too, offset by an intriguing tartness and a stubbornness that had kept her climbing all day. No wonder she was tired!

Without quite realising what he was doing, Campbell reached out to smooth the tumbled hair from Tilly's cheek. The silkiness of her curls and the smoothness of her skin were like a physical shock, and he withdrew his hand sharply.

Better have that stew, he told himself.

He took the video camera with him as he backed out of the tent. God only knew what Tilly had been saying to the camera before she had fallen asleep. Knowing her, it might have been anything! He had better make sure there was something sensible on there.

Campbell finished the stew, cleaned out the pot and his plate, and turned his attention to the camera. Clicking it on, he cleared his throat.

> 'This is Campbell Sanderson. We're camped on the shoulder of Ben Nuarrh, so if we leave at zero six hundred tomorrow morning we should be in a position to make it to the summit in good time. It's been a successful day, after a slow start. I didn't feel that Tilly was taking things very seriously to start with, but she's done well this afternoon. Very well, in fact.'

There, that ought to do it. Campbell decided that he had been concise, accurate and generous. He hadn't said anything about how long it had taken to coax her down the abseil, or about the stupid fuss she had made about jumping over a few stones to cross the river. He had carefully refrained from commenting on her lipstick or on how unfit she was. He had said nothing about her bizarre flights of imagination.

And nothing about her smile, nothing about the teasing humour in her dark blue eyes, or her infectious laugh.

Nothing about her enticing softness as she'd pressed up against him on one of those boulders.

No, he wouldn't be saying any of that. Campbell switched off the camera with a sharp click.

CHAPTER FOUR

'OLIVIER?' Tilly struggled out of a deep sleep to find herself pressed up against a solid male body.

It was pitch dark. Disorientated, she tried to prop herself up on one elbow and her stiff muscles screamed in protest, jerking her properly awake with a gasp.

Campbell was instantly alert. 'What's the matter?'

That wasn't Olivier's voice. Tilly blinked at the darkness for a moment until her brain kicked in and she remembered where she was, and just who she was cuddled up against.

Campbell Sanderson.

'Ouch!' Her sore muscles pinched again as she moved hastily away from him. Between her stiffness and the sleeping bag, it was hard to move at all.

'It's you,' she said, dismayed.

'I'm afraid so.'

Tilly was attempting to disentangle herself from her sleeping bag. The wind was howling and shrieking around the tent and she could hear an ominous drumming on the canvas. Rain. Just what you wanted when you were camping.

'What time is it?' she asked blearily.

'Two-fifteen.'

'How on earth do you know that?' She had seen no tell-tale

luminous watch face and there was no way he could have seen the time without a light.

'I just do.'

Her silence was obviously eloquent with disbelief, for he sighed and switched on a pencil torch, pointing it at his watch. 'Satisfied?'

Tilly peered at the watch face. 'Two-sixteen,' she read.

'It was two fifteen when you asked me.'

His calm certainty riled her. 'I bet you were checking your watch under the sleeping bag just before I woke up.'

'Of course. I've spent all night awake in the hope that you would wake up and ask the time so that I could trick you.'

Her lips tightened at his tone. 'Well, how did you do it, then?'

He shrugged. 'I've got a clock in my head. It's years of training. There are times when you need to know the time but can't afford to switch on a light.'

Tilly tried to imagine what it would be like to be in a situation where you couldn't risk putting on a light. She would never be able to cope. She was a terrible coward.

'Presumably nobody is going to ambush us up here, so can I have the torch again?' she asked as she wriggled awkwardly out of her sleeping bag at last.

'Where are you going?'

'I thought I'd pop out and get a DVD.'

'*What?*'

She sighed. 'Where do you think I'm going?'

'Oh.' He sounded exasperated. 'Can't you hang on until morning?'

'No, I can't. My bladder hasn't had years of training. I'll never be able to get back to sleep until I've been.' She groped around for her boots. 'Can you point the torch while I put these on?'

With a long-suffering sigh, Campbell directed the beam of light. 'You'll need a jacket, too. It's raining.'

'What did I do with it?' wondered Tilly, patting the end of her sleeping bag. It was hard to see anything with just a fine pencil beam of light. 'I was so tired I can't remember taking it off.'

'You didn't. I undressed you last night.'

It was Tilly's turn to do a double take. 'You did *what*?'

'Don't worry,' said Campbell dryly. 'I didn't even enjoy it. You were dead to the world and I'm not into necrophilia. I stopped at your dungarees. I thought they might be a bit tricky to take off without some cooperation from you.'

Tilly flushed in the darkness, imagining him grunting with effort as he manhandled her out of her clothes. No wonder he had stopped! The poor man had probably been exhausted.

That was the story of her life, she thought glumly. An attractive man undressed her and she wasn't even awake to appreciate it.

She didn't bother to lace her boots. It sounded like a wild night out there and she wasn't planning on being very long.

Yelping at her sore muscles, she took the torch and struggled out of the tent only to find herself staggering against a gust of wind that slashed rain across her face. Straightening as best she could, she saw that it was very dark, and she began to wish that she had hung on after all. There might not be enemy soldiers lurking behind the outcrops, but it took her imagination no time at all to sketch out the beginning of a horror story. The sooner she got back into the tent, the better.

Tilly did her business as quickly as she could, which wasn't very fast, given that her fingers were numb with cold. The skiing dungarees might be warm, but she had forgotten just how long it took to unfasten them. It was all right for Campbell, with his no doubt highly trained bladder.

She was wet and shivering by the time she scrambled back into the tent and zipped up the entrance once more. Then she had to go through the whole business of taking off her jacket and boots again. She put the torch on the sleeping bag where the beam was promptly buried until Campbell picked it up and held it for her so that she could see what she was doing. Tilly was grateful, but very conscious, too, of how close he was. It felt very intimate, being together in such a confined space, and, although she did her best to stick to her sleeping bag, it was impossible not to touch him.

'I can't believe people do this kind of thing for fun,' she grumbled through chattering teeth. 'Who'd want to camp when you could be tucked up in an nice, cosy B and B? God, I'm freezing!'

'Your hair's wet,' said Campbell. Incredibly, he had a smallish towel in his hand. 'Turn round and I'll dry it for you.'

'Where on earth did you find that?' Tilly asked to distract herself from his nearness as he rubbed her hair vigorously.

'In my pack.'

'That's not a pack—ouch!—that's a bottomless pit!'

'I came prepared for the conditions,' he said. 'I knew there was a good chance we'd get wet somewhere along the line.'

'Pity you didn't bring a hot shower,' muttered Tilly. 'You seem to have everything else in there.' Her ears were sore and she tried to pull her head away, but Campbell kept a firm grip on her. 'Ow!' she protested. 'That hurts—and God knows what my hair's going to look like in the morning.'

'It's more important that you don't go to sleep again with wet hair,' he pointed out, giving her hair a final rub before tossing the towel aside. 'There. Get back in your sleeping bag and you'll soon warm up.'

Shuddering with the cold, Tilly clambered back into the bag and pulled the covers tight under her chin. 'How soon is soon?' she asked, unclenching her jaw after a few moments. 'I don't suppose you thought to bring a hot-water bottle?'

She heard a sigh through the darkness, and the next moment Campbell had rolled over and was pulling her bodily towards him, sleeping bag and all, making her squeak with surprise. 'You'll have to make do with body heat,' he said. 'You can't beat it when you're cold.'

He shifted to make himself more comfortable and put an arm over her, tucking her firmly into the curve of his body. 'Now, have you quite finished fidgeting?' he asked, his astringent tones at odds with the warm reassurance of his hold.

'Yes.' Tilly's voice was huskier than she wanted.

'Then perhaps we can both get some sleep?'

Sure, but how could she be expected to sleep when his arm was heavy over her and she could feel his breath stirring her hair? Even through two sleeping bags, she was desperately aware of his solid male warmth.

In spite of her exhaustion, Tilly had rarely felt less like sleeping. All her senses were on high alert and fizzing away as if they had had ten coffees apiece. She could hear the rain drumming overhead while the wind plucked angrily at the canvas. The tent smelt of canvas and hillside and wet jackets.

It was strange to be lying next to a man again, and Tilly was surprised at how right it felt with Campbell's arm around her. There had been no one since Olivier.

Olivier... How desolate she had been when he had dumped her! Tilly had done her best to hide her humiliation behind a bright and breezy exterior and she thought she had done a good job of convincing everyone that she was over him, so it had come as something of a shock to realise that even her brothers, never very perceptive when it came to emotions, had realised how miserable she was inside.

'You need to meet someone new,' they had told her. 'It's time you got out there and started looking instead of hiding away in your kitchen.'

'I'm not hiding away! I've got a business to run, and it happens to involve a lot of time in the kitchen, that's all.'

Even her friends had started. 'Olivier wasn't the one for you. The right man is out there somewhere, Tilly, but you won't meet him stuck at home. You've got to go out and find him.'

Tilly hadn't believed them. She knew none of them had liked Olivier particularly, but she had been so in love with him, so utterly convinced he was The One. What was the point of looking for Mr Right when she had already found him, and discovered that she couldn't have him? Tilly hadn't wanted to meet someone new. All she'd wanted was for Olivier to come back and tell her that it had been a terrible mistake, that he did love her after all. That was all she had dreamed about for months now.

The odd thing was that now when she closed her eyes, she couldn't picture him clearly. Tilly frowned into the darkness. Oh, she remembered what he looked like, of course she did, but his image was strangely two-dimensional, like a photo in a magazine. When she tried to bring it into sharper focus, all she could see was Campbell: Campbell looking exasperated, Campbell shaking his head in disbelief, Campbell smiling that unexpected smile that made her pulse kick just remembering it.

Perhaps the boys and all her friends would shut up now, Tilly hoped. They had got their way. Between them, they had bullied her out of the kitchen and halfway up a Scottish mountain, and sure enough she had met someone new, even someone available.

But Campbell was no Mr Right, and even if he had been looking for Ms Right, which she doubted very much, it was clear that Tilly wasn't at all what he would have in mind.

How could she be? She had known him for less than twenty-four hours, but it took a lot less than that to realise that he was a man determined to have the best of everything. She hadn't been at all surprised to hear that his ex-wife was dazzling. Campbell Sanderson would never accept that anyone else could do better than him. So any woman on his arm would have to be the most beautiful, the wittiest, the cleverest, the best-dressed.

Tilly was none of those things. No way would a man like Campbell ever want someone who muddled through life and looked a mess most of the time while she was doing it. Olivier hadn't wanted her either.

No, she should just accept that she was never going to be a woman men desired or cherished. She was resigned to being good old Tilly now—the good friend, the one men went out with if they wanted a break from adoring their high-mainte-nance women and needed an evening of fun with no strings attached.

Not that Campbell would even want that. He was too chilly and driven to relax with a jolly evening in the pub. He wasn't the type to want a shoulder to cry on either. Look at how he had clammed up the moment she had suggested that he might have loved his wife.

How he must have hated losing her to another man. Of course, anyone would find it devastating, but it would be the losing that would really rankle with a man as competitive as Campbell. He wasn't the type to shrug his shoulders and accept a situation. He certainly wasn't the type to make do with second-best, Tilly decided, and that was the most she could ever be. Frankly, she would be lucky to make second-best. Those keen green eyes missed nothing, and she wouldn't be at all sur-prised if she had ranked as a non-starter.

Well, that was OK, Tilly told herself. He didn't have anything *she* wanted either.

All right, maybe that wasn't *quite* true. He had a great body and an unexpectedly attractive smile, but any Mr Right of hers would need a lot more than that. Tilly had no intention of humiliating herself any further by not reaching Campbell's impossible standards. She had never matched up to her father's, had failed to meet Olivier's, and she was sick of feeling inadequate, she decided. There was only so much rejection a girl could take.

No, if Harry and Seb thought their plan to drag her out of the kitchen would lead her to Mr Right, they were in for a disappointment.

Tilly was prepared to admit that she found Campbell attractive, but that was as far as it went. She wouldn't be letting her defences down or getting her expectations up.

On the other hand, since she was here, being held tight against that hard body, it would be silly not to enjoy it, wouldn't it? Tilly closed her eyes and snuggled closer to Campbell. She might as well make the most of it.

'Time to get up.' Campbell touched Tilly on the shoulder to wake her, but she only groaned and turned away from his hand to bury her face in her sleeping bag.

He shook her harder. 'Come on, wake up. We've got a mountain to climb.'

Tilly groaned louder. 'Climb it yourself,' she mumbled.

'Unfortunately, I can't do it without you,' said Campbell. 'Come on, get up. I've made you some tea. You can drink it while I'm packing up the tent.'

Tilly was tempted to tell him what he could do with his tea, but Campbell was already rolling up his bag and stuffing it into his pack. Clearly he wasn't going to let her rest until she was up and out.

Grumbling, she climbed blearily out of the tent and straightened, only to freeze as she found herself staring at a view that was literally breathtaking. The rain had stopped some time in the early hours and the chilly wind had blown away all the clouds, leaving a pale luminous sky suffused with sunrise. Great golden brown hills rolled away into the purple distance, without a single sign of human habitation. No roads, no telegraph poles, no electricity pylons. Just rocks and heather and a lone bird calling somewhere above them.

'Oh,' she said.

'Quite something, isn't it?' Campbell poured tea into an enamel mug. 'Now, aren't you glad you got up?'

'Ecstatic,' said Tilly sourly, grimacing as she tried to straighten her back. Awe-inspiring it might be, but it would take more than a view to improve her mood. 'I love being bullied awake at the crack of dawn and dragged outside to drink tea in the freezing cold halfway up a mountain when I'm so stiff I can't even stand up straight! I mean, it's the perfect way to start a day. Who wants to wake up in a big, wide bed with sun striping the crisp white sheets as some gorgeous man brings in a tray laden with fresh coffee and croissants and apricot jam when you could be here?'

Campbell handed her the mug of tea with a mixture of incredulity and amusement. 'You've only been awake two minutes, woman! It's too early for fantasies.'

'It's never too early to fantasise about food,' she told him. 'Especially when you missed supper. Is there any breakfast? I'm starving.'

'Well, I can't provide coffee and croissants, but otherwise I can fulfil all your fantasies,' said Campbell, and Tilly looked hopeful. *'Really?'*

'Here.' He produced a cereal bar from his pocket and offered it to her.

She took it suspiciously. 'What is it?'

'It's a high energy bar. You'll need it to get you up to the top.'

Unwrapping it, she took a cautious bite. 'Disgusting,' she pronounced, chewing madly.

'Hey, you wanted breakfast, I gave you breakfast.'

'You're going to have to work on the fantasy thing,' said Tilly, still chewing.

'I will if you'll work on the getting going thing,' said Campbell pointedly. 'Roger and Leanne are probably already on their way.'

'I bet they're not. I bet Roger is being nice and letting Leanne have a lie in after walking so far yesterday.'

'More fool him.' Campbell bent back to the tent and hauled the two packs outside before starting to pull out the tent pegs. 'He'll never win by being nice.'

'No chance of catching *you* making that mistake,' Tilly said acidly, and he looked up at her with a fleeting grin.

'I never make that mistake,' he said.

Jarred anew by the effect of a smile on that wintry face, Tilly looked away. She almost wished he wouldn't do it, especially not when she had just decided that he was impossible and how glad she was that she wasn't his type.

She busied herself looking in her pack for a toothbrush instead, and took her empty mug to the burn so that she could clean her teeth. She felt a little better after that, at least until she found a tiny folding mirror.

Aghast at her reflection, she went back to Campbell, who was dismantling the tent poles with his customary efficiency. 'Why didn't you tell me I looked like a dog's breakfast?'

He glanced up briefly. 'What's the problem?'

'Look at my hair! That was you messing it up last night,' she accused him. 'And my face!'

Dismayed, she peered into the mirror once more, hoping that the red welt across her cheek might have miraculously disappeared. She had obviously been lying with her face pressed against the zip of the sleeping bag. It didn't make for a good look, particularly not when combined with eyes that were piggy with tiredness and hair that resembled a straggly bird's nest. There were probably things nesting in there already.

And the final touch—a smear of mud left over from her splat landing on the river bank. She rubbed at it grouchily but that only seemed to make it worse.

'It doesn't matter,' said Campbell, not knowing what all the fuss was about. She looked fine to him. A little tousled, maybe, but he thought that dishevelled, just-fallen-out-of-bed look suited her.

Unfortunately, his attempt to sound soothing didn't appear to have worked. 'It does matter!' Tilly was scrabbling in her pack for a hairbrush. 'There'll be cameras at the other end. I don't want to go down in posterity looking like this!'

Campbell sighed. 'Can we worry about that when we get there? Look, I promise you can have a primping stop on the way down, but let's just get to the top first.'

Forcibly removing the hairbrush from her hand, he made her put everything away again. By the time she had finished, the tent was neatly folded up and stowed away in his rucksack. He picked up her pack, helped her into it and adjusted the straps for her as if she were a child.

'OK,' he said and pointed up to the summit that loomed above them. 'Let's get up there.'

Tilly craned her neck to follow his finger and her heart sank. 'I'll never be able to do it! I can hardly walk!'

Campbell swung his own pack on to his back. 'You'll feel better when you get going.'

Annoyingly, she did. It was steep going, though, and they had to scramble up the last bit.

'I can't do it,' Tilly kept wailing, her breath coming in ragged gasps as she clung to a rock or clutched at a clump of heather, but Campbell wouldn't listen.

'You can.'

And, in the end, she could. It was an amazing feeling as she climbed the last few feet and stood on the summit, looking down at the magnificent hills spread out at her feet. Tilly felt her heart catch with awe.

'Wow,' was all she could say.

Campbell was watching her face. He had deliberately waited so that she would get to the top first. 'See what you can do when you try?' he said as he joined her.

'It's amazing!'

It was. It was like discovering yourself poised on the edge of a brand new life—one you never imagined you could have. A smile spread over her face and she stretched out her arms as she spun slowly, savouring her achievement. 'I can't believe I did it!'

'And you got here first,' he reminded her.

'Unless Roger and Leanne have been and gone?' Tilly suggested. She looked innocent, but the blue eyes were dancing with mischief.

Campbell didn't rise to the provocation. 'They're still on their way up,' he said with satisfaction, and pointed down to where they could make out two tiny figures toiling up the slope.

'Looks like Leanne got a lie in after all,' said Tilly. 'We should wait and say hello.'

'We'll do no such thing,' said Campbell. 'We haven't won yet. We'd better get something on camera to prove we were here, and then we're on our way down.' He got the camera out and checked it. 'Ready?'

'Hang on, just let me put some lippy on…'

He rolled his eyes. 'For God's sake, Jenkins!' he said impatiently. 'We're on top of a mountain. This is no place for lipstick!'

'It is if I'm going to be on film.'

Tilly peered into her mirror, squinting so she didn't have to look at her hair or the smudges of mud, and carefully outlined her mouth with her favourite cherry-red. It was extraordinary what a bit of bright lipstick could do for the morale. She had always wanted to be able to do the natural look but the fact was that she suited bright colours.

Campbell had been setting up the camera on an outcrop and was squinting through it while he waited impatiently for her to finish. 'If we sit on that rock, it'll get us both in. Might be a bit of a squash, but it'll be quicker than two separate sessions.'

They perched together on the rock, and Campbell put his arm round her to keep them both in frame. 'Smile!' he muttered out of the corner of his mouth. 'And say something for the camera.'

Burningly aware of his arm, Tilly smiled. 'Here we are on the top of Ben Nuarrh and it feels as if we're on top of the world,' she told the camera and gestured around her. 'It's the most beautiful morning.'

She drew a deep breath. 'I can't believe that we got here at last,' she confessed. 'I feel incredible! I never believed that I could do it, and I probably wouldn't have done if Campbell hadn't bullied me all the way,' she said with a glance at him. 'I'm glad you did,' she added almost shyly.

'That's not what you said this morning!'

'No, well, I was tired this morning,' said Tilly with dignity. 'I hardly slept at all.'

Campbell pretended to gape in astonishment. 'You most certainly did!'

Forgetting the camera, she turned to look at him. 'I didn't snore, did I?' she asked anxiously. She had been worried about that.

'I wouldn't call it a *snore*, exactly. There was quite a bit of snuffling and grunting and smacking of lips. It was like sharing a tent with a rather large hedgehog.'

'Charming!' Tilly made to thump him but she was laughing, elated by the morning and the mountain top and the fizzing awareness of his presence.

'Other than that,' he said, 'I very much enjoyed sleeping with you.'

That was when she made the mistake of looking into his eyes. They were the same pale, piercing green but alight with humour and something else that made Tilly's laugh falter suddenly.

She moistened her lips. 'Do you think that's enough for the camera?' she asked, and Campbell's gaze held hers for a moment longer.

'I think it probably is.'

For the umpteenth time, Tilly rearranged the wooden spoons by the hob and then snatched back her hand with an exclamation of annoyance. 'Oh, for heaven's sake!' she said crossly. She was driving herself mad!

The television crew were due any minute. Tilly told herself she was just worried about having cameras in the house, zooming in on all the undusted mantelpieces, but deep down she knew that the prospect of seeing Campbell again was the real reason she was feeling so jittery.

It was three weeks since they had stood on the top of Ben Nuarrh. Campbell had marched her down the mountain in record time to make sure that they won the first stage, so they were ahead on points. Winning, however, was by no means a foregone conclusion. He still had to complete his challenge first, and then the viewers would have a vote after seeing clips from the video diaries and filming, so they wouldn't learn the final result until a grand awards ceremony later in the year.

Remembering Campbell's frustration at realising how much depended on the vagaries of the viewers' reactions, Tilly smiled wryly. He was so obviously a man who liked a clear goal, a definite mission that he could go out and accomplish. Want a bridge blown up? A hostage rescued? A mountain climbed in record time? Campbell was your man. But all this waiting to see what people thought and felt was not for him. Having started, though, he was committed to finishing now or it really would feel like failure.

And failure wasn't something Campbell Sanderson was prepared to contemplate, that was clear.

So he would be arriving any minute now to learn how to design and make a wedding cake, and he would be determined to succeed, however little he might enjoy it.

Well, she hadn't enjoyed abseiling, Tilly remembered, or crossing that river. *Or* being bullied up and down that mountain! It had been wonderful at the top, of course, and she was very glad that she had done it in the end, but she wasn't at all anxious to repeat the experience. She had been very happy to come back to her cosy kitchen—or rut, as Harry and Seb would call it— and she was looking forward to being the one who knew what she was doing this time.

How was Campbell going to react to *that*? Tilly didn't see why she should make it too easy for him. He had made her suffer, after all.

After the elation of making the summit, he had been brisk on the way down, and clearly couldn't wait to tie up the formalities at the end and get away. Tilly had been a little hurt by that, even though she knew it was silly. It wasn't as if either of them had wanted to be there. Nothing had *happened*.

It was absolutely ridiculous to be missing him, in fact.

'So, what was he like?' her best friend, Cleo had asked, brushing aside details of Tilly's traumatic abseil and homing straight in on the man assigned to partner her. 'Attractive?'

Tilly thought about the glint in Campbell's green eyes, about his mouth and that smile and the strength in his hands. She had barely known him forty-eight hours, and it was vaguely disturbing that she could still picture him in quite such detail.

She decided to downplay all that, though. Cleo would never

let her forget it if she thought Tilly had found herself alone in a tent with an attractive man and done absolutely nothing about it.

'Quite,' she said, deliberately casual. 'In an I-could-show-some-emotion-but-then-I'd-have-to-kill-you kind of way.'

'Ooh…' Cleo brightened. 'He sounds gorgeous!' Her eyes sharpened. 'Available?'

'He's divorced,' Tilly admitted reluctantly.

'I think you should go for it.'

Tilly felt oddly ruffled. 'I wouldn't stand a chance. Besides, he wasn't really my type. He wasn't anything like Olivier.'

Which was true. Olivier had been dark and passionate, while Campbell was all cool containment. It was hard to imagine two men more different, in fact.

'All the better,' said Cleo, who hadn't liked Olivier. 'Someone not like Olivier is exactly what you need.'

'I don't need Campbell Sanderson,' said Tilly definitely. 'I've never met anyone so competitive—unless it's my father! All men like that care about is winning,' she went on with a touch of bitterness. 'Never mind whose feelings they might be trampling on their way to success.'

'You don't need to spend the rest of your life with him, just have a bit of fun. Boost your confidence after that toad, Olivier.'

Tilly shook her head so the brown curls bounced around her face. 'I can't imagine anything *less* likely to boost my confidence,' she said frankly. 'Campbell is someone who has to have the best of everything, including women, and I don't see me falling into that category, do you?'

'You are the best,' said Cleo loyally. 'You're funny, generous, warm, caring and sexy, if only you'd admit it. And you're a fabulous cook. What more does a man want?'

'A size six with legs up to her armpits?'

Cleo clicked her tongue. 'You are so screwed up about your weight, Tilly! Listen, you are *not* overweight, you're just curvy.

That's the way women are meant to be, and that's how most men like them if the truth be told. Why do you think their tongues hang out whenever they spot a cleavage? You're never going to be a stick insect, true, but you shouldn't just accept that, you should celebrate it!'

'Maybe I would if I could just lose a stone,' said Tilly, reaching glumly for the biscuits. 'Anyway, don't get your hopes up about Campbell Sanderson. He's hung up on his ex-wife, if you ask me, and I don't want to get involved with that again. I had enough of being a consolation prize with Olivier.'

'Then why not think of Campbell as *your* consolation prize?' Cleo suggested.

The more she thought about it, the more Tilly had begun to wonder whether Cleo might have a point. She was overdue a good time, after all. She deserved a treat, and it wasn't as if she would have any expectations. A brief affair to boost her ego and make her feel good about herself again—was that so much to ask?

Then Tilly would catch a glimpse of herself in a mirror and she would catch herself up, appalled at her presumption. What was she *thinking*? There was no way Campbell would be interested in her, even if she laid herself out on a plate for him.

Anyway, she was probably building him up in her mind, she reassured herself. When she saw him again, she would probably wonder what she had made all the fuss about and be very glad that she hadn't made a fool of herself.

CHAPTER FIVE

EXCEPT it didn't work out like that. The moment Campbell came through the door, Tilly's heart gave a sickening lurch into her throat, where it lodged, hammering so hard she could hardly speak.

He was exactly as she remembered him, but somehow more so. Everything about him seemed very definite, and she was aware of him in startling detail, down to the buttons on his shirt, the fine hairs on his wrist, the faint line between his brows as he watched the crew bustling around the kitchen, talking about light and angles.

Momentarily sidelined with him, Tilly cleared her throat and forced her heart back into position. 'How have you been?'

'Busy,' said Campbell succinctly. 'I'm moving to the States in three weeks, and there's a lot to do before then.'

So he clearly wasn't going to have time for a little seduction on the side.

Tilly told herself that it was just as well. Her confidence was so low that he would be boarding his plane before she got up the nerve to try a little light flirtation. She had never been any good at that.

Anyway, look at him, so cool, so detached, so self-contained. It was all very well for Cleo to talk about having fun, but how could she have fun with a man like Campbell? It would be like trying to have fun with a granite rock.

No, forget it, she told herself. Just do the programme. Think about Mum and what this could do for the hospice. Teach him how to make a cake and don't for one second let him think you might even have considered the possibility of fun!

There was a pause. It didn't seem to bother Campbell but the silence made Tilly uncomfortable. 'Where are you staying while you're here?' she asked, hating how inane she sounded. The two of them had shared a tiny tent. They had laughed on top of a mountain. She had clung to him and begged him not to let her go. And now she was treating him as if he were a stranger she had met at a cocktail party.

If Campbell noticed the incongruity of it, he made no comment. 'In a hotel,' he said. 'The Watley...' He twiddled his hand to indicate that he had forgotten the rest of the name.

'The Watley Hall.'

'You know it?'

'Everyone here knows the Watley Hall, even if we can't afford to eat there. It's the best hotel in Allerby.'

She might have known that was where he would be staying.

'It's not very enterprising of you,' she commented tartly. 'I thought you would be pitching a tent in the garden!'

Campbell glanced at her. His face was perfectly straight but there was a glimmer of a smile at the back of his eyes, and her heart tipped a little, as if she had missed a step.

'Sorry to disappoint you, but I'm just a boring businessman nowadays, wanting a place to work.'

'I thought you were supposed to be learning how to make a wedding cake?'

'During the day,' he agreed. 'I will need to catch up with work in the evenings, so a hotel will suit me rather more than a tent. And you'll no doubt be glad to know that I'll be out of your hair once the baking lesson is over for the day.'

The baking lesson. Tilly didn't miss the dismissive note in Campbell's voice, and her eyes narrowed. He obviously thought cake-making was a trivial business, easily mastered. A token few minutes in the kitchen every day and then he would be planning to head back to his hotel room to deal with real man's business!

They would see about that.

Campbell was looking around the kitchen. He had somehow imagined Tilly living in a muddle, but although the room certainly had a relaxed feel to it, with a couple of comfortable old armchairs at the far end, he was relieved to see that it was clean and very well-organised. From what little he had seen of it so far, the whole house had a friendly, welcoming air.

'This is a nice house,' he commented. 'There must be more money in cakes than I thought.'

'Sadly not,' said Tilly dryly. 'This was my stepfather's house. My mother and I moved in here when I was seven. Mum died when I was twenty, and Jack the following year, so the mortgage was paid off. We spent quite a lot of time at the hospice over those couple of years,' she explained with a little sigh. 'I suppose that's why it means so much to me.'

'How old were your brothers then?'

'Only twelve,' she told him. 'Jack made me their guardian before he died so I could keep this as a home for them. We'll have to decide what to do with it when they reach twenty-five. If they ever settle down, Harry and Seb may want to sell so they can buy their own places, but there's no sign of them doing anything remotely sensible yet, so until then I'm happy to stay here.'

Campbell was watching her with a slight frown in his cool eyes. 'Don't you get a say?'

'It's not my house. Seb and Harry aren't going to throw me out in the street, so it's not as if I'm going to be destitute or anything.'

'Still, it seems strange not to have made any allowance for you,' said Campbell, surprised at how concerned he felt on her behalf. 'I know you were just a stepdaughter, but presumably Harry and Seb are your half-brothers. You're family.'

'Don't blame Jack,' said Tilly loyally. 'At the time it was the reasonable thing to do. My real father is still alive and has much more money than Jack ever had. Of course Jack assumed that I would be well provided for.'

'And you're not?'

Tilly looked away. 'I asked my father for help after Jack died. We had the house, but most of Jack's money was tied up in trust for the boys' education, and I didn't know how I was going to manage with day-to-day expenses.'

'Surely your father didn't refuse to help you?'

'No, not exactly,' she said. 'He offered me a home, college fees if I wanted them and even an allowance, but he wasn't prepared to take on the twins. I don't think he ever forgave my mother for being happy with Jack,' Tilly went on thoughtfully. 'Even though *he* was the one who left *us*, for a new wife more in keeping with his oh-so-successful image,' she added with a touch of bitterness. 'Mum wasn't supposed to be happier than he was after that.'

Campbell's brows contracted. 'So he made you choose?'

'That's right. I could be his daughter or I could be the twins' sister, but I couldn't be both.' She smiled wryly. 'At least it wasn't a difficult decision to make!'

'Wasn't it?' he said. 'Not many twenty-one-year-olds would turn their back on financial support in favour of looking after two boys.'

'What was I supposed to do? Walk away and leave them to bring themselves up?'

'They must have had other family who could have looked after them.'

'There was Jack's sister, Shirley, but she was much older than Jack, and she'd never had any children. I'm not sure if she would have been able to cope with the twins, and it would have been awful for them, too. She was very strict and used to get terribly anxious about noise and mess, two things you can guarantee a lot of with twelve-year-old boys around!

'They'd lost so much,' Tilly remembered sadly. 'First Mum, and then Jack. I was all they had. I wasn't going to abandon them.'

She was watching the television crew moving around the kitchen, but the deep blue eyes were sombre and it was clear that she was lost in memories. Campbell found his gaze resting on her face, on the dark sweep of her lashes and the curve of her cheek. She had beautiful creamy skin, the kind you wanted to touch, to see if it was as warm and soft and lush as it looked.

He had thought about her much more than he had expected over the last three weeks. The oddest things would trigger a memory and he would be back on that hillside with Tilly. Campbell had been surprised at how vividly he could picture her, how precisely he remembered the scent of her hair, the feel of her squashed against him, the curve of that generous mouth and the sound of her laughter.

Most of all, he remembered how he had felt when he was with her. Her sparkiness had made him uneasy, and he had been torn between exasperation and feeling reluctantly intrigued by the contrast between her warm, sensuous body and her tart humour.

Looking at Tilly now, Campbell realised that there was a stubbornness and a strength to her, too. He could imagine her squaring her shoulders and bearing the burden of her young brothers' grief as well as her own. It couldn't have been easy looking after the two of them.

'You were very young for that kind of responsibility,' he commented.

Tilly shrugged, her eyes still on the cameraman. 'Lots of girls are mothers before they're twenty-one,' she reminded him.

'Not of twelve-year-old boys.'

'Maybe not, but I just had to get on with it. People deal with a lot harder things every day.'

Yes, stronger than he had thought.

'Still, it must have been hard. At twenty-one you should be off exploring the world, enjoying yourself, finding out what you really want to do with your life.'

She smiled slightly at his determination to feel sorry for her. 'I know what I really want to do,' she said. 'I'm doing it now.' She gestured around the kitchen. 'I worked in an office for a few years. It was a dull job, but it paid the bills and meant I could make a home for Harry and Seb while they were at school, but when they went to university I could suit myself, and that's when I decided to set up Sweet Nothings.'

Campbell was looking dubious. A cake-making business was all very well, but she was clearly an intelligent woman.

'You didn't want to do something more…?'

'More what?'

'More…' He searched for the right word, and failed to find it. '…challenging?' he suggested at last.

As soon as the word was out of his mouth, he knew he had blundered. Tilly was smiling, but there was a flinty look in her eyes.

'No,' she said levelly. 'I love what I'm doing. How can one ask for more than that?'

Fortunately Suzy came over just then. 'I think we're ready,' she said. 'Tilly, can you show Campbell the kitchen and explain what he's going to have to do for the camera, then we'll leave you to get on with it. Have you arranged about the wedding cake, by the way?'

'Yes, a friend of mine called Cleo has agreed to let Campbell make hers. She's got a good sense of fun and she won't be traumatised if it's all a disaster.'

'When's the wedding?'

'A week on Saturday.'

'Perfect. We'll come and film you both with the cake then. It should make a great scene!'

Campbell was expressionless as Tilly showed him round the kitchen and then opened her portfolio of designs. She had made cakes in an extraordinary range of designs, from Manolo Blahnik shoes to giraffes to a golfer driving off a tee.

'As you can see,' she said for the benefit of the camera, 'here at Sweet Nothings we make whatever the customer wants. It's important that they feel that their cake is unique, so I spend quite a lot of time talking to them first, about who the cake is for, and what exactly they want to celebrate.'

She turned a page and the camera zoomed in over her shoulder, missing the real story, which was the tightening of Campbell's jaw as he realised just what he was getting into.

'Some people want a fun cake, perhaps to fit in with the theme of a party, or with a particular interest. You'd be amazed what some people are interested in, so you need to be adaptable. So if you had to make a cake for someone with a really strange hobby—an interest in Roman military history, say—' she said, unable to resist the dig at Campbell, 'you'd have to do some research to see what a soldier in the legions might have worn, for instance.'

Campbell was looking wooden, and Tilly suppressed a smile. 'Fortunately, there aren't too many odd-bods like that around,' she went on innocently. 'Most people are normal.'

That would teach him to sneer at baking.

For the benefit of the camera, she turned a few more pages. 'Some customers prefer a more traditional cake, but they still want the personal touch. The main thing to remember is that I'm making the cake they want, not the cake I think they should have. You'll have to bear that in mind when you make Cleo's wedding cake.'

Campbell managed to unclamp his jaw. 'Has she decided what design she wants yet?'

'No, she's coming in tomorrow to talk to you about that. You can discuss it together.'

Campbell couldn't see *that* conversation lasting long. He didn't have the slightest interest in wedding cakes, as Tilly clearly knew only too well. How the hell was he supposed to come up with a design for a wedding cake? There hadn't even been a cake at his own ill-fated wedding to Lisa.

He eyed Tilly suspiciously, wondering if she was deliberately setting him up, and when she pulled a pink apron emblazoned with 'Sweet Nothings' from a drawer, he was sure of it.

'You'll need to wear this when you're baking and decorating,' she told him, and he recoiled, his expression everything Tilly had hoped for.

'I'm not wearing that!'

'I'm afraid you'll have to,' she said sweetly. 'Health and safety regulations.'

'Do put it on,' Suzy urged from behind the camera. 'The viewers will love it!'

Campbell opened his mouth to tell her in no uncertain terms what she could do with her viewers when he caught sight of Tilly's face. Her eyes were alight with laughter.

'You planned this!' he muttered out of the corner of his mouth.

'Only in the way you planned that river crossing,' she whispered back.

'It'll win you so many votes,' Suzy promised. 'Roger was none too happy about putting on a special uniform to do the pedicure either, but the viewers do love a good sport.'

'Does Roger have to wear pink?' Campbell asked sourly, but he tied the apron round him. This whole experience was going to be humiliating enough without letting Roger outdo him. It would take more than an apron to beat him.

Folding his arms, he glared at the camera. There was a long moment of utter silence while Tilly, Suzy and the cameraman all looked at him, and then there was a muffled snort as Tilly broke first.

She couldn't help it. Campbell looked so ridiculous, glowering over the pink pinny. On a man who would be utterly at home in camouflage and a black balaclava, the apron looked positively bizarre and his expression was so forbidding that she started to laugh.

A moment later Suzy joined in, too, and then the camera was shaking as Jim, the cameraman, succumbed as well. They laughed and laughed while Campbell regarded them with a jaundiced expression, not at all amused.

'I didn't realise you were making a comedy,' he said caustically.

'Oh, dear.' Suzy wiped her eyes and made an effort to control her giggles. 'I'm sorry, but this is just perfect! The contrast between you two couldn't be better!' She sighed happily. 'This is going to be *such* a great programme. All you've got to do is make that cake now, Campbell—oh, and don't forget your video diaries again!'

'Boy, that Suzy knows how to manage you,' said Tilly as they waved the producer and cameraman off at last.

Campbell scowled as he snatched off the apron. 'What do you mean?'

'She knows she just has to dangle the prospect of Roger winning in front of your nose and you'll do anything to beat him, even if it means wearing a pink apron!'

'I'm certainly not going to make myself look ridiculous unless I *do* win,' said Campbell trenchantly.

'Campbell, has it ever occurred to you that you might lose?' Tilly asked, folding her arms and studying him curiously. 'Someone has to.'

'Not me,' he said. 'I never lose.'

'Your ex-wife might not agree about that,' Tilly couldn't help retorting. 'You don't have a very good success rate when it comes to relationships.'

He shrugged that aside. 'Relationships are different.'

And clearly a lot less important than winning as far as Campbell was concerned.

Tilly remembered Cleo's advice to have a little fling and sighed. Campbell was far too focused on winning this competition to waste any time on her. She could stand on the table and do the dance of the seven veils until she was stark naked, and Campbell would be telling her to stop wasting time, they needed to get on. He was only here now because he couldn't win without her.

'Come on,' she said, resigned. 'If you're going to win, we'd better get on with teaching you how to make a cake. Have you ever done any baking before?'

Campbell was still fuming about the apron episode as he followed her back to the kitchen. 'No, but surely it's just a question of reading some instructions?' he said irritably.

'Oh, good point.' Tilly paused and put her head on one side as if struck by his good sense. 'I never thought of that. Well, that'll save us some time. Why don't you go ahead and make one, then, and I'll put the kettle on? We probably won't need to bother with the rest of the week. We'll just have half an hour on icing tips before the wedding, and you can spend the rest of the time working.'

He eyed her for a moment, certain that she was testing him

somehow, but then again, how difficult could it be? It was only a cake, for God's sake!

'All right,' he said, accepting her unspoken challenge. Unconsciously, he squared his shoulders. Not only would he make a cake, he would make the best cake she had ever tasted. If she thought mocking his interest in the Romans and dressing him in pink would put him off his stroke, she would soon discover that she was mistaken!

'Don't forget your apron,' she reminded him.

Setting his jaw, Campbell retrieved the apron and looked around for a recipe. The dresser held a whole range of cook books and he had no idea where to start. Only the knowledge that Tilly was just waiting for him to admit that he could do with some advice made him pull out a book at random.

Favourite Cake Recipes... Just what he needed. Campbell turned the pages determinedly, although his heart sank as he was presented with yet more choices. Who would have thought that there were that many different kinds of cake?

Eventually he settled on a chocolate sponge cake with butter icing. It looked like the ones his mother had used to make when he was a boy and she had knocked them out in no time.

'I'll do this one,' he said, showing Tilly the picture.

'Great,' she said. 'I love chocolate cake. You'll find cake tins in that drawer there, dry ingredients in the larder—over there—and everything else in the fridge. Off you go, Sanderson!'

He looked at her, suspicious of her enthusiasm. 'What are you going to be doing?'

'Oh, I'll be here working on a few designs,' she said, plonking herself down at the table. 'Feel free to ask if you can't find anything.'

Campbell set about his task with grim determination. Working his way down the list, he managed to assemble all the ingredients, but the eggs were cold, the butter hard and he had obviously dismissed the difference between caster and granulated sugar as irrelevant. Tilly could practically see him thinking *flour is flour is flour* before deciding that plain flour would do just as well as self-raising, and he picked out a cake tin at random without any thought for its size or whether or not it needed to be lined.

It was odd that a man so focused, so competent, so coolly logical, should have such a cavalier approach to baking, she thought. But then, Campbell wouldn't see cooking as important, would he?

Still, she had to give him marks for perseverance. He got points for tidying up, too, after he had put the cake in the oven. 'There,' he said at last, laying the cloth out to dry on the edge of the sink at a precise right angle. 'That's done.'

Realising that he was still wearing the stupid apron, he wrenched it off and tossed it aside.

Tilly was sitting at the end of the table, idly turning the pages of a magazine, and he eyed her sardonically.

'Working hard?'

'I am, as a matter of fact,' she said equably. 'I'm researching. I've got clients coming in to choose a twenty-first birthday cake for their daughter, so I want to be able to give them some fun ideas. I do a lot of bags and shoes, but I'm wondering if I might do a complete outfit like this one.' She turned the magazine so Campbell could see the photograph she was considering.

He looked at it uncomprehendingly. 'Why don't you just make her a nice chocolate cake?'

'Because anyone can do that—even you, apparently! I'm offering something different, and I can't do that unless I've got a real sense of the person the cake is for. Actually, making the cake is the easy part. You need to be able to talk to people, and listen to what they tell you.'

She fixed him with a stern gaze. 'That means when Cleo

comes in tomorrow you can't just fob her off with a traditional three tier cake. You need to find out what kind of wedding she's planning, what sort of cake she really wants, and come up with some ideas for her. Cleo's my friend, and she's agreed to let you do her cake as a favour to me, so you've got to make it really special for her.'

'You'll be there, too, won't you?' Campbell asked with a touch of unease. He couldn't imagine having much to say to an excited bride full of wedding plans. 'I'm not very good at talking at all, let alone about that kind of stuff.'

'I wasn't any good at abseiling, but I still had to do it,' Tilly pointed out tartly. 'Yes, I'll be there, just as you were at the top of the cliff, but I can't do it for you. This time it's your challenge.'

Campbell sighed. 'Why does it have to be so complicated? A cake is a cake!'

'When you were in the army, were all operations the same?'

'I was in the Marines, but no, they weren't.'

'And now you're in business, is every deal exactly the same?'

'No.'

'Well, it's the same with cakes.'

Tilly could see that he wasn't convinced. 'Every time I make a cake, I'm making it for different people, and a different situation. Even if they choose exactly the same cake, the way I mix it and bake it and decorate it is all different. If it wasn't, my customers might as well go to a supermarket and buy one made in a factory.'

'The next time I'm negotiating an important deal I'll think of you and remind myself that it's just like a cake,' said Campbell dryly.

Tilly couldn't help warming to the idea that he might be thinking about her in the future. 'Will you have to do much of that in your new job?'

'Negotiating? I imagine so. This will be my most challenging job yet. I'm going to a global corporation that's been on a downward slide for some time. I've been appointed to turn it round, but it won't be easy.'

'Oh, but surely it's just a question of reading some instructions?' Tilly murmured provocatively.

Campbell looked at her sharply. She met his gaze blandly, but the dark blue eyes gleamed and, in spite of himself, he laughed.

'It would be nice to think that there would be some instructions to read!'

Tilly found herself smiling back at him, even while wishing that she hadn't made him laugh. It was so obvious that Campbell thought that making cakes was beneath him that she had been doing a good job of disliking him again, and now he had gone and spoilt that by smiling.

All at once she was tingling with awareness again and, instead of thinking about how arrogant and disagreeable he could be, she was thinking about the fact that the two of them were alone in the house, and trying not to notice how tall and lean and tautly muscled he was, how out of place he seemed in the cosy kitchen with that air of tightly leashed power.

Looking at him in that pink apron, Tilly had the unnerving sensation that she had tied a bow around a kitten only to realise that it had turned into a fully grown tiger, complete with swishing tail, and she only just stopped herself from gulping.

She pushed back her chair so that it scraped on the tiles. 'Tea?' she asked brightly.

'Thanks.'

Campbell sat down at the table and pulled her sketchbook towards him. As he flicked idly through it, his brows rose. Her designs were quick and clear, and she had somehow captured each idea in a few clever lines.

'These are good,' he said, unable to keep the surprise from his voice.

Tilly switched on the kettle and turned to lean back against the sink, determinedly keeping her distance.

'It's not exactly turning round a global corporation, is it?'

Campbell turned another few pages. 'I'm beginning to wonder if that might not be easier than coming up with ideas like these.'

'Well, that's why you're a hotshot international executive and I'm the provincial cake-maker,' said Tilly. 'If you think about it, we don't have a single thing in common, do we?'

Campbell looked at her standing by the kettle. Her nut-brown curls gleamed with gold under the spotlights, and he remembered how soft her hair had felt under his cheek as they had lain together in the tent up on the Scottish hillside. Funny to think they had only spent a matter of hours together. She seemed uncannily familiar already. Campbell wasn't a fanciful man, but it felt as if he had known the glint of fun in her eyes, the tartness of her voice, the gurgle of laughter, for ever.

'No, I don't suppose we do,' he agreed, his voice rather more curt than he had intended.

And they didn't. Tilly was right. They had absolutely nothing in common.

It hadn't taken Campbell nearly as long as he had expected to adjust to civilian life. He had always been too much of a maverick to fit that comfortably into naval life, even within an elite unit. An unorthodox approach and a relentless drive to succeed at whatever cost came into their own on special operations, but were less of an advantage in the day-to-day routine.

He hadn't regretted leaving all that behind. Lisa hadn't intended to change his life for the better when she'd walked out, but he was grateful to her in an odd way for making him so determined to prove that he could make twice as much money as her new husband that he had gone into business. It had turned out that he was made for the ruthless cut and thrust of corporate life. Campbell didn't do emotions, or talking or any of the things women thought were so important, but he knew how to make money, and that was what counted.

When it came down to it, Campbell believed that everybody was motivated by money at some level. Tilly wouldn't agree, he was sure. That was *another* thing they didn't have in common.

'We just have to get along for a fortnight with nothing in common,' he said. 'Then I'll be gone.'

Thanks for the reminder, Tilly thought, piqued in spite of herself. It was all very well deciding not to get involved with him, but quite another thing to be hit over the head with the fact that he was planning to leave the country soon. She had a nasty feeling he had done it to make sure that she got the message that he wasn't available. Why didn't he just hang up a sign saying 'don't bother'?

Not that she had any intention of letting him know that she had even *considered* the possibility of getting involved. That really *would* make him laugh.

'Of course, you're moving to the States, aren't you?' Tilly was Ms Cucumber Cool as she carried the teapot over and found two mugs. She could do couldn't-care-less as well as anyone, even Campbell Sanderson. 'Where exactly are you going?'

'New York.'

'Is that where your ex-wife lives now?'

Campbell looked at her, startled. 'How do you know that?'

'Well, you said she lived in the States, and you don't seem the kind of man who lets go easily. I wondered if you were going there because you wanted to see her.'

'Not at all,' he said sharply. 'It just happens that's where the head office is.'

Infuriatingly, though, Tilly's words had made him pause and examine his own motives for the first time. 'Of course I've considered the chance that I might bump into her,' he went on after a while. 'New York is a big city, but Lisa's new husband is in a similar line of business, so it's not beyond the bounds of possibility that we'll meet.'

'Gosh, I hope he's not more successful than you,' said Tilly, only half joking, and Campbell smiled grimly.

'Not any more,' he said.

CHAPTER SIX

TILLY poured the tea. She could just imagine how Campbell would have been driven to out-perform the man who had taken his wife away from him. It would have hurt anyone, but to a man like Campbell the implication that she had left him for someone more successful must have been an extra dose of salt in the wound.

'What will it be like, seeing her again?' she asked.

He shrugged, and she rolled her eyes as she pushed a mug across the table towards him.

'Come on, you must have thought about it! I've spent the last eighteen months practising what I would say to Olivier if I ever saw him again—not that I've had the chance to say any of it,' she added ruefully. 'It's probably just as well.'

'Olivier?'

'The beat of my heart for two years,' she said, blue eyes bleak with memory.

And presumably the man who had taught her that the absence of children didn't make a break-up any easier. Campbell was remembering now.

'Ah,' he said. Were commiserations in order? These kinds of emotional conversations always made him uncomfortable. He couldn't understand why women insisted on talking about this kind of stuff the whole time.

'What *would* you have said?' he asked at last, opting for a practical approach.

Tilly thought about it. 'It depended on the mood I was in,' she said. 'Sometimes I was determined to make him realise just what he'd lost, so I was going to pretend to have a fabulous new lover and carry on as if I'd almost forgotten him. At other times I wanted him to acknowledge how he'd hurt me, but either way I would be very cool and calm.

'In reality, of course, if I *had* bumped into Olivier, I would have burst into tears and begged him to come back, and then none of my friends would ever have spoken to me again!'

Campbell studied her across the table. Her generous mouth was twisted in a self-deprecating smile, but the blue eyes were wistful, and he wondered what Olivier was like. Campbell didn't like the idea of him at all. He didn't like the idea of anyone hurting Tilly.

She wasn't beautiful, not like Lisa. Her features were too quirky for that, but there was something alluring about her all the same, he realised. She had warmth and wit and a charm that Lisa had never had, and in a strange way she was sexier, too.

The thought was startling, but Campbell decided it was true. Lisa was slender and elegant and perfect, but she was a woman most men admired from a distance. Tilly was quite different—all soft curves and luminous skin—and there was something irresistibly *touchable* about her. Any man's fingers would be twitching with the need to reach out and slide through her hair, to smooth and stroke and explore that warm, lush body, and then he would want to take that mouth and see if it tasted and felt as good as it looked...

Alarmed by how quickly his thoughts had drifted out of control, Campbell slammed on the brakes and gave himself a mental slap.

He drank his tea, feeling jarred and vaguely uneasy. Tilly was the one with the vivid imagination, not him. Campbell Sanderson was famous for his coolness under pressure, for his single-minded pursuit of a goal. He wasn't a man who let himself get distracted, especially not by a woman. The last time that had happened, he had ended up married to Lisa, and look what a mistake that had been! No way was he doing that again.

'If you cried, there really would have been no chance of getting him back,' he said caustically to make up for the fact that while his mind was firmly back under control, his hands were taking rather longer to catch up and were still tingling at the idea of touching Tilly.

Scowling at the sign of weakness, Campbell gripped them firmly around the mug.

'I know.' Tilly sighed. 'What is it with men? Look at you. You're happy to jump off a cliff but show you a woman in tears and I bet you'd run a mile!'

This was unfortunately so true that Campbell could only glower. 'I like dealing with facts,' he said. 'Emotions are messy.'

Tilly stared at him and shook her head. 'How on earth did you ever manage to get married in the first place? You must have had to succumb to a teensy little emotion then, surely!'

'The attraction between us was a physical thing. It was never about hearts and flowers and all that stuff. Lisa's not like that. She's like me in lots of ways. She knows what she wants, and she goes after it, and she gets it. And for a time,' he said, 'she wanted me.'

Campbell paused, remembering. 'It's hard to resist a woman who looks the way she does. You'd have to see her to understand,' he said, catching Tilly's sceptical expression.

'I can't see you being pushed into doing anything you didn't want to do, let alone marriage,' she said. 'You're not the passive type.'

'No,' he admitted. 'I did want to marry her.'

'Because you loved her, or because you could show her off, prove that you had a more beautiful wife than anyone else?'

A very faint flush stained Campbell's cheekbones. 'I suppose there's some truth in that,' he acknowledged. 'But marriage was Lisa's idea. I'd never imagined myself as a marrying type, but she wanted a wedding, and I was mad for her. I didn't care what happened as long as I could have her. I should have known it wouldn't last.'

What would it be like to be so beautiful you always got your own way? Tilly wondered. What would it be like to be desired so much by Campbell that he would do whatever you wanted?

'How long were you married?' she asked instead.

'Just three years,' said Campbell. 'There was great sexual chemistry but not much else going for the marriage. I was away on operations most of the time, and Lisa wasn't prepared to sit at home waiting for me. She liked to have fun, and she liked money, and it didn't take her long to get bored and start to want something more glamorous. Arthur offered her the lifestyle she wanted, so she took it.'

He shrugged, but Tilly couldn't believe that he was as nonchalant about the failure of his marriage as he pretended. It must have been a huge blow to his pride.

'Are you hoping that if she sees how successful you are now, she might come back to you?'

Campbell stared at her for a moment, then pushed the mug abruptly aside. 'No,' he said instinctively, and then, honestly, 'I don't know.'

So what were you thinking, Tilly? Tilly asked herself. That he might say, *Of course not, how could I possibly want my beautiful ex-wife with whom I shared such incredible sexual chemistry when I could have you for a brief fling?*

'I was angry when she left,' he said unexpectedly, almost as if the words had been forced out of him. For a long time all I thought about was seeing Lisa again, and making her regret the choice she had made. I probably did hope that she might change her mind then.'

'And now?'

'Now…now I think I want her to see what she could have had if she had stuck with me. Beyond that, I really don't know. I probably won't know until I do see her again.'

Well, she had asked and he had answered. Tilly couldn't complain that he hadn't been honest. She was very glad that she hadn't done anything silly, like taking Cleo's advice. Campbell was like a dog with a bone that it had tired of until the moment someone tried to take it away. Losing Lisa to another man would smack too much of failure for a man like him. Consciously or not, Tilly was prepared to bet that his life since then had been focused on getting his wife back.

Perhaps that was how it should be, she thought, but it was hard not to feel a little disconsolate. No one would ever feel that way about *her*. Olivier certainly hadn't, she remembered with a trace of bitterness. Even if she had been the one to dump him, he would probably just have been relieved that she had saved him the trouble. He wouldn't still be hankering after her four years down the line.

She should just face up to the fact that she wasn't the kind of girl men got possessive or obsessed about, Tilly decided glumly. She had better just stick to baking.

And, talking of which…She sniffed delicately and looked across at Campbell, who was staring into his tea with a brooding expression.

He glanced up as he felt her eyes on him. 'What?'

'How long has your cake been in?'

'The cake!'

Campbell leapt to his feet and yanked open the oven, only

to cough and splutter as smoke billowed into his face. Grabbing a tea towel, he pulled the tin out, swearing as he burned his fingers and let the tin fall with a clatter on to the work surface.

When the smoke cleared, he could see that the cake was not the perfect chocolate cake he had intended to make. Instead, it was burnt, hard and flat. It didn't take a Michelin starred chef to see that it was going to be inedible.

Only the tiniest of smiles dented the corner of Tilly's mouth as she went into the larder and found a banana cake she had made a couple of days earlier. She put it on the table and sat down again, very carefully saying absolutely nothing.

'All right!' snarled Campbell as if she had been shouting accusingly at him. 'All *right*! It's not just a question of reading the instructions, OK? I admit it! Happy now?'

He looked so chagrined at his failure that Tilly had to bite her cheeks to stop herself from laughing out loud.

'Actually, it *is* just a question of following a recipe,' she tried to placate him, 'but you have to know how to read it first. I can teach you that.' She cut him a slice of cake. 'Here, try a bit of this.'

Campbell took a bite. It was a revelation—moist and light and delicious, its flavours and textures perfectly balanced. He felt as if he had never eaten cake before. He finished the slice without speaking and then looked straight at Tilly. 'That was the best cake I have ever tasted,' he said simply.

She laughed, pleased. 'That's one of the easiest cakes to make. You can try one for yourself tomorrow if you like.'

'I suppose there's some secret ingredient you keep to yourself to make sure no one else makes a cake as good as yours.' Campbell looked at her accusingly, but Tilly held up her hands in a gesture of innocence.

'I promise you there isn't. Pleasure in food is for sharing, not keeping to yourself.'

'There must be something special you do.'

'Oh, there is,' she agreed. 'I make all my cakes with love. Do you think you'll be able to do that?'

There was a tiny silence as their eyes met across the table.

Campbell was the first to look away. 'Will determination do instead?'

'If that's the best you can offer, we'll have to hope it's good enough for Cleo's cake.'

Cleo was dark and vivacious and she eyed Campbell with undisguised interest when she arrived to discuss her wedding cake the next day. Right at home in Tilly's kitchen, she plonked herself down at the table and proceeded to cross-examine him with all the subtlety of a sledgehammer while Tilly made coffee.

Campbell wasn't doing a bad job of deflecting her questions, Tilly thought as she put a plate of biscuits she had made earlier on the table between them, but if he had hoped to deter Cleo he was in for a disappointment.

'Biscuits…yummy…and Tony's favourites, too! Can I take some home for him?'

Without waiting for an answer, Cleo turned back to Campbell.

'Tilly's a fabulous cook! Well, you probably know that already, Campbell.' She leant confidingly towards him. 'Tony was wild with envy when he heard you were going to be spending a couple of weeks here. He's always angling for an invitation to dinner and then he spends weeks afterwards asking me why I can't be a domestic goddess like Tilly.'

Ignoring Tilly's warning kick under the table, she sat back and warmed to her theme.

'Lucky she's such a special person or I'd really hate her. As it is, everyone loves Tilly,' she told Campbell. 'She's the best friend anyone could have. She's the one we all go to when we need looking after. I don't know what I'd do without her, and I certainly don't know what Harry and Seb would have done without her. She brought them up, you know. She's a born mother, I think, and she's going to make some lucky guy a perfect wife one day.'

Tilly sighed and gave up on trying to be discreet. It was way too late for that now. The only thing she could do now was to brazen it out. 'Why not come right out and offer Campbell fifty camels if he'll take me off your hands?' she asked acidly. 'You'll have to forgive Cleo,' she said to Campbell as she handed out mugs of coffee. 'Wedding bells have gone to her head. Just because she's getting married, she thinks everyone else should be, too. She's desperate to get me attached to some poor unsuspecting man and she doesn't care who she embarrasses to do it! Just ignore her.

'And you, Cleo,' she added, pointing a stern finger at her friend, 'stop it! Campbell is here to make your wedding cake, and that's it. He isn't attracted to me and I'm not attracted to him.'

Cleo was quite unabashed. 'We wouldn't have to embarrass you if you ever made the slightest effort to find someone new. You just hide yourself away in this kitchen and nobody ever knows what a lovely person you are. Honestly, it's a crime! *Tell* her, Campbell.'

'I am not hiding away!' said Tilly, exasperated, before Campbell had a chance to reply. She dropped into the chair next to him. Right then, he seemed to be her only ally. 'Nobody seems to understand that I'm trying to run a business here! Tell *her*, Campbell!'

Campbell looked from Tilly's heated face to Cleo's amused one, and his lips twitched. He had, it was true, been a little taken aback by Cleo's blatant matchmaking, and wasn't at all sure how he should react, but Tilly's intervention had dispelled any awkwardness.

She was right, of course. He *wasn't* attracted to her. Interested, perhaps. Amused, even intrigued, but not attracted.

Not really. Not the way he had been attracted to Lisa, anyway, and the two women were such polar opposites that it would be bizarre to find them both attractive. Still, Tilly's bluntness had stung a little. She had made him feel a fool for being so aware of her the day before.

When he had taken himself back to his hotel at the end of the day, Campbell had told himself that he was relieved, but the truth was that his room had seemed cold and empty and sterile somehow after Tilly's house. He had opened his laptop determinedly and tried to concentrate on work but his famous ability to focus had completely deserted him. He'd found himself reading emails without taking in a word, while his mind had drifted back to Tilly moving around the bright kitchen.

In her own context, her movements were graceful, her hands quick and competent. Campbell had found it strangely restful to watch her. Alone in his hotel room, he had pictured her in disconcerting detail, pushing her hair back from her face, rolling her eyes, smiling her crooked smile. She had a way of running her tongue over her lips when she was thinking. It was quite unselfconscious, and Campbell wondered if she had any idea how sexy she was, or how it made him think about what it would be like to lose himself in her warmth and her softness and her light.

'Campbell?' Tilly waved a hand in front of his face. 'This is Earth calling! Do you receive?'

Campbell snapped to, aghast to discover that he had been lost in his thoughts and that Cleo and Tilly were staring at him. He was supposed to be trained to be alert at all times. He could just imagine his Commanding Officer's scathing comments if he had caught him sitting there daydreaming about a woman! A faint flush of embarrassment crept up his cheeks.

'Sorry,' he said gruffly, remembering what he was supposed to be doing. 'I think it's probably better if I don't get involved. That way you can both carry on believing you're right.'

'A little weasely, but tactful, I suppose,' said Tilly in a dry voice. She pushed the biscuits towards her friend. 'Have one of those and give up on the matchmaking! And now that's sorted, let's get down to business.'

'I thought we were doing just that,' said Cleo, who had been watching Campbell's face with amusement.

'Your *cake*,' Tilly reminded her, exasperated. 'That's why you're here, in case you've forgotten! This is supposed to be a business meeting. Have you had any thoughts about it? Or have you been too busy meddling in the lives of all your single friends?'

'No, I've been thinking about it and I've even consulted Tony,' said Cleo with a grin. 'The wedding service and the reception immediately afterwards are going to be traditional—it wasn't worth fighting Mum on that one—but we want the party in the evening to be fun. What do you think about an Antony and Cleopatra theme?' She looked hopefully at Campbell. 'Could you make a cake like that?

Campbell glanced at Tilly for help, but she just looked blandly back at him. 'Antony and Cleopatra?' he repeated carefully.

'Yes, you know, like the Shakespeare play. I mean, how can we resist? My name really is Cleopatra, can you believe it? I don't know what my parents were thinking of!' Cleo shook her dark head, but her eyes twinkled. 'It's just chance that I fell in love with an Anthony, but it's a cool coincidence, don't you think?' She struck a melodramatic pose. 'Another pair of legendary lovers!'

'Correct me if I'm wrong, but don't Antony and Cleopatra

die at the end of the play?' said Campbell dryly. 'It doesn't seem much of a precedent for a wedding cake.'

'Details, details.' Cleo waved that aside. 'We just want all the fun bits. Egypt, eyeliner, bathing in milk, you know the kind of thing.'

Eyeliner? Ye gods. Campbell had to resist the urge to bang his head on the table.

'None of that sounds very suitable for a cake,' he told her austerely, and Tilly dug a finger into his ribs.

'What did I tell you about listening to the client?' Her voice was bubbling with suppressed laughter. 'If Cleo wants an Antony and Cleopatra cake, that's what she can have.'

She turned to Cleo. 'I can't believe I've never made the connection between Tony and Anthony before! I think it's a brilliant idea, Cleo. I did the play for A level and loved it. There's no reason why we—Campbell, I mean—can't make a cake for you. It could be the alternative version: Antony and Cleopatra, happy ever after.'

'That's what I thought.' Cleo nodded eagerly. 'Antony and Cleopatra going off on their honeymoon, perhaps?'

'On their barge…wasn't there a barge in the play?'

Cleo clapped her hands together. 'Oh, yes, of course. The barge!'

'And they could have tin cans tied on the back, and a card saying "just married"!'

'And our names and the date of the wedding along the side.'

'*Yes*. This is going to be great!' Tilly gave Campbell another prod. 'Are you noting all this down, Campbell?'

Campbell felt as if he were at a tennis match, his eyes shifting from side to side as he tried to follow the ideas bouncing backwards and forwards between them.

He looked at the notebook in front of him. 'You want me to make a *barge*?'

'An ancient Egyptian one. You're bound to be able to find a picture on the Internet somewhere. Antony was a Roman so you'll be able to do him OK, and Cleopatra will be easy—give her black hair, big fringe, lots of eyeliner.'

And he was supposed to make all this out of *cake*?

Campbell listened as Tilly and Cleo carried on sparking ideas off each other, talking at dizzying speed, laughing and egging each other on. 'We mustn't forget the asp!'

He couldn't help comparing this with the business meetings he was used to, where he told people what he wanted done and they did it. The meetings he chaired were much more controlled, much more efficient.

Much less fun.

'What do you think, Campbell?' Tilly had been drawing a quick summary in her sketchbook and she twisted it round so that he could see. He leant closer, trying not to notice the summery scent of her hair.

'Very clever,' he said. 'I would have just stuck a couple of figures on top of a cake.'

'Yes, well, that wouldn't have won you many votes, would it?'

Campbell straightened. He had forgotten about the competition there for a while. Which was odd, given that winning it was the only reason he was here.

'They're bound to be impressed by this, if you can do it,' said Cleo. 'It does look a bit complicated, though. Would you rather we came up with a simpler design, Campbell?'

'No, that's fine,' he said, unable to admit that he didn't have a clue where to start with it, but was determined to succeed at this the way he succeeded with everything else. 'Tilly promises her clients that they can have whatever cake they want, so if this is what you want, Cleo, this is what I'll make you.'

'Wonderful!' Cleo beamed as she got to her feet. 'It's going to be such fun! You will stay for the party after they've filmed the cake, won't you, Campbell? Once they've gone, you and Tilly can relax and enjoy yourselves—separately if you want,' she added, rolling her eyes in such exaggerated resignation at Tilly's expression that Campbell couldn't help laughing.

Normally the thought of a wedding made him run in the opposite direction, but Cleo was so friendly that he didn't want to hurt her feelings. Besides, he had to go anyway to deliver the cake. It would be his last evening with Tilly.

'Thanks,' he said. 'I'd like to come.'

'I'm sorry about that,' said Tilly as she came back from seeing Cleo off. She dropped into a chair with a sigh. 'I hope Cleo didn't embarrass you. She certainly embarrassed me! Sometimes I feel like disowning all my friends!'

'I liked her,' said Campbell. 'And she's obviously very fond of you.'

'I know.' Tilly dragged the hair back from her face with both hands. 'She's a good friend, but she's got it into her head that I need a man. And it's not just Cleo! It's a conspiracy,' she complained. 'Even my brothers are in on it, so be warned. Seb and Harry are both coming home for the weekend and, as neither of them know the meaning of subtlety, you'll probably find yourself tied up and forced into bed with me!'

A tiny smile tugged at the corner of Campbell's mouth as her regarded her. 'I can think of worse fates.'

Dark blue eyes flew to meet his for a fleeting moment before she looked away and coloured. 'You don't need to be polite,' she muttered.

'I'm not. You're an attractive woman. You must know that,' he said with a frown as Tilly goggled at him.

She swallowed. 'It's not how I think of myself, no,' she said at last.

'Why not?'

'Isn't it obvious?'

'I don't understand why you're so hung up about your

weight,' said Campbell with a touch of exasperation. 'OK, so you're not the thinnest woman I've ever met, but you look absolutely fine to me. Some women aren't meant to be thin, and you're one of them. It's only women who get worked up about what size they are. Men don't care.'

'I notice they all like to go out with thin women, though,' said Tilly waspishly as she got up and began clearing away the mugs. 'I bet your ex-wife is slim, isn't she?'

'She ought to be. She never ate anything. It was a waste of time taking her out to dinner,' Campbell remembered.

'I wish I could be like that!'

'But then you wouldn't have had your fantasies about meals to get you up Scottish mountains,' he pointed out. 'You wouldn't be you.'

'No, I might be slender and elegant and controlled.'

There was no mistaking the bitterness in her voice as she turned and began rinsing the mugs at the sink.

Campbell looked at her back. 'That sounds very dull,' he said carefully, forgetting that Tilly's chaotic quality had once made him uneasy, too. 'Who on earth would want you to be like that?'

'Olivier did.' Tilly was still clattering mugs and wouldn't turn round. 'That's why he broke off our relationship in the end. I couldn't be the kind of person he wanted me to be. I was too much for him.'

'Too much what?'

'Too much everything, I think. I ate too much, laughed too much, talked too much, loved too much…' Her back was still firmly turned and, even though she was clearly trying to keep her voice light, Campbell could still hear the undercurrent of pain.

'Surely those are the reasons he would want to be with you in the first place?'

'I don't think it was like that for Olivier. Cleo's theory was that I was a kind of project for him. Perhaps he saw me as

some kind of challenge. Maybe he thought it would be interesting to see if he could shape me into something different,
someone cool and controlled who would blend with his stylish
décor.

'But of course I never could blend in,' Tilly went on, setting
the mugs on the draining rack and turning at last. 'Now I feel
ashamed for trying to, but I loved him so much, I was desperate to please him. I'd have done anything he wanted, but I just
couldn't be that different. I'm just not like that.'

Her throat was tight with remembered hurt, and she couldn't
bear to meet Campbell's eyes. She reached for a tea towel
instead and wiped her hands very carefully.

'In the end, I think Olivier found me disgusting,' she said
with difficulty, her gaze on the tea towel. 'It was awful. The
more I tried to please him, the more he withdrew. It was as if
he couldn't bear me near him.'

Campbell heard the crack of pain in her voice and anger
closed like a fist around his heart. 'Who was this guy?' he
demanded furiously.

'He's an architect. A very good one. He's moved to London
now. I think Allerby was too provincial for Olivier.'

'Or maybe he was too affected for Allerby,' Campbell suggested. 'What can you expect with a poncey name like Olivier?'
he demanded. 'I suppose his real name is Oliver and he wanted
to make himself more interesting.'

Tilly couldn't help feeling touched that he was so angry on
her behalf, but habit drove her to defend Olivier.

'His mother's French,' she told him. 'That's why he's Olivier
and not Oliver. Actually, the name suits him. He's very dark and
good-looking and…oh, *glamorous*, I suppose,' she remembered with a sigh. 'He was always out of my league. He's not
just handsome, he's clever and witty and artistic and good at
everything he does.'

'He certainly did an excellent job of destroying your self-confidence,' said Campbell acidly.

Tilly smiled a little sadly. 'I don't think I've ever had much of that, not when it comes to men, anyway.'

Her hands were as dry as they were ever going to be. She made herself hang the tea towel back on its hook and opened the fridge to look for butter and eggs. When in doubt, Tilly always baked. There was something about the process that soothed her. She had made an awful lot of cakes in the months since Olivier had decided she was never going to match up to his standards.

Campbell pushed back his chair to watch her. 'Why not?'

'Cleo blames my father, but then Cleo would. She's an amateur psychologist. She says that I'm "replicating a pattern of loving men I can't trust".' Tilly hooked her fingers in the air to emphasise the quotation.

'And are you?'

She shrugged as she searched for sugar, flour and sultanas in the sliding larder.

'I don't know about that, but whatever it is I do, I'm not doing it again,' she said. 'It wasn't just Olivier. Before him it was Andrew, and before *him*, Simon. They weren't quite as demanding as Olivier, but I'm sick of not being quite good enough. I'm sick of having my heart broken.'

Carrying the dry ingredients over to the table, she started to set them down and looked at Campbell at last. 'I know my friends mean well. I *know* they just want me to be happy. They think I shouldn't let Olivier put me off men for life, and that I should just get back out there and start dating again, but I don't dare. I'm too afraid I'll just end up getting hurt again.'

She stopped, the packet of sultanas still clutched against her chest. 'Funny, I've never admitted that to anyone else,' she said, a puzzled crease between her brows. 'I must feel safer with you than I thought.'

'I'm not sure that's very good for my ego,' said Campbell wryly, and she flushed a little, belatedly realising that she had spoken her thoughts aloud.

'I just meant…because you're only here for a week,' she tried to explain. 'You're not just leaving Allerby, you're leaving the country soon, so even if we did find each other attractive, a relationship would be out of the question.'

CHAPTER SEVEN

RIGHT, and he needed to remember that, Campbell told himself that night. He was surprised at how much he had hated seeing how hurt Tilly had been by Olivier—and he didn't care what she said about him being half-French, it was still a damn fool name.

What a sinful waste that she should have cut herself off from men. Alone and restless, Campbell scowled up at the ceiling through the darkness. He badly wanted to show Tilly that she was wrong, that she was quite beautiful and sexy and desirable enough as she was.

But how could he do that without hurting her himself?

Tilly had told him that she was afraid, and he didn't have time to win her confidence. Even if he did, what then?

He was moving to the States, Campbell reminded himself. Taking over a company with a global reputation like Mentior's would be the culmination of his business career. There would be no stopping him now. He was going to take that firm and turn it round and make it the best in the world again, and he was going to do it where Lisa couldn't fail to note his success.

Ever since Lisa had left him, he had been focused on proving to her just how big a mistake she had made. He would never have a better chance than this. There was no question of not going.

And that meant there was no question of convincing Tilly

that she was a desirable woman. She was absolutely right. It was best for both of them if they kept their relationship firmly on a friendly basis. Tilly had made it very clear that was all she wanted.

He needed to be realistic, after all, Campbell told himself. They were only together because of the television programme. As soon as Cleo's wedding was over, and he had made that cake, they would go their separate ways. They would meet up at the awards ceremony for one last filming and, if they had won, as Campbell fully intended they would, they would hand over their cheques to the hospice that meant so much to her, and that would be that.

It was impractical to even think about anything else.

Unfortunately, that didn't stop Campbell thinking about it anyway. It was hard not to when he and Tilly were spending so much time together.

Campbell hadn't expected to enjoy his time learning to make cakes. He had expected to be bored and impatient to get back to the office. He checked his email regularly, and his PA had strict instructions to ring him if there were any problems, but they all seemed to be managing perfectly well without him, and Campbell found himself thinking about work less and less and about Tilly more and more.

Never having given it any thought, he had been surprised at quite how much was involved in making cakes for a living. As Tilly explained, it wasn't just a question of baking. She had long interviews with each client to find out exactly what they wanted, then the cake had to be designed and decorated and delivered on time. She sourced recipes, shopped for ingredients and priced each cake, but what she was best at was talking to people.

Inclined to be dismissive at first, Campbell came to recognise her ability to make connections for the skill it was. He watched clients relax as they sat at Tilly's table and told her about who or what they wanted to celebrate with a special cake, and he watched their faces when they saw what Tilly had made for them.

There were almost always gasps of pleasure and admiration when the cake was unveiled, and he could understand why. Campbell was amazed at what she could do. The day after Cleo's visit, she had made a football pitch complete with players in the correct strips for a nine year-old boy who was a Manchester United fan. Campbell had helped her deliver it to the birthday party and would have enjoyed the whole experience if he hadn't had to drive a van with 'Sweet Nothings' painted on the side.

A *pink* van.

Campbell had told Tilly she needed to work on her corporate image, but she'd just laughed at him. 'Everyone loves the pink van,' she said. 'It's fun.'

'I just hope to God nobody I know sees me in it,' he grumbled and Tilly slid him a mischievous glance.

'Perhaps you're the one who needs rebranding,' she suggested. 'You could tone down all that macho man and get in touch with your feminine side!'

The look Campbell sent her in reply made Tilly laugh out loud.

'OK, there *is* no feminine side. That would explain why you're finding it so hard to make a cake!'

And Campbell had to admit that he was struggling on that front. Tilly made it look so easy, but when he'd tried to make even a basic sponge it was a disaster.

'Look, it's not a competition,' Tilly said to him, watching him square up to his ingredients for yet another practice cake. 'It's not about winning, or beating the ingredients into shape. It's magic.'

She let some caster sugar run through her fingers, caressed a speckled brown egg. 'It's about taking all these different ingredients and turning them into something that looks wonderful and smells wonderful and tastes wonderful. You're too aggressive,' she scolded him. 'You're treating cooking as a battle, with you as Julius Caesar and the ingredients as the poor old Britons! Don't think of the recipe as a series of manoeuvres. Think of it as helpful advice to create something beautiful.'

But, frustrated by his inability to master baking the way he had mastered every other obstacle in his way, Campbell was too brisk, too impatient for results, to do anything of the kind. He didn't know what Tilly meant when she said it wasn't about winning. Why else would he be making a fool of himself like this?

He was much happier sorting out her office for her and criticising her accounting system. He fixed wobbly shelves and changed the light bulbs she couldn't reach. He checked the oil in the van and filled up the windscreen wash. He set up a special business email account for Sweet Nothings.

'If you carry on like this, I'm not going to want you to leave,' Tilly said.

Leave. Campbell was jolted by the reminder. Of course he would be leaving. He would be getting on a plane and flying off to the States, where there would be no Tilly humming tunelessly as she moved around the kitchen. No Tilly endlessly teasing him about his military approach or his interest in Roman history. No Tilly there rolling her eyes, wearing her bold bright lipstick, leaning forward with an animated face, encompassing everyone she talked to in her warmth and her light.

But he would be in New York. He would be successful. He would look Lisa in the face and show her everything that she had lost.

'Careful!' Tilly cautioned him as he lifted the cake out of the back of the van. 'This one's very fragile.'

Campbell looked down at the cake, decorated to look like a bed complete with pink frills, scatter cushions and a teddy bear. It was covered with cosmetics, a chick flick DVD and a sparkly top.

'Is this a birthday cake?'

'It's for a sleepover party.'

To Campbell the house seemed full of shrieking, giggling girls who flocked around them, exclaiming at the cake and tossing back their hair as they cast sidelong glances at him under their impossibly long lashes while Tilly carried on an in-depth conversation with the birthday girl's mother.

'Phew!' He let out a long breath when he finally managed to extricate her and made an escape. 'I'd rather parachute into enemy territory than do that again.'

Tilly rolled her eyes in a characteristic gesture. 'Honestly, they were just a few little girls!'

'They weren't little, and they were terrifying. You could have warned me!'

'I didn't realise that it would be quite such a traumatic experience for you,' she said, grinning as she unlocked the van. 'You certainly weren't much back-up support!'

'Hey, I got you out of there, didn't I?'

'I'm not sure grabbing me by the wrist, telling Jane that we had to go and dragging me to the door really counts. You might try a more diplomatic approach next time.'

'There's going to be a next time?' said Campbell, his horror only half feigned.

'Perhaps I'd better make it solo missions if there's any girly stuff involved,' said Tilly, laughing at him over the roof of the van. 'I hope this never gets back to the mess. The day Campbell Sanderson panicked when confronted with six twelve-year-old girls!'

'I did not panic,' he said, trying to suppress an answering grin. 'I merely made a strategic retreat. I was thinking of you, in any case,' he added virtuously as they got into the van. 'It's been a long day.'

Tilly stretched and sighed. 'It has. At least that's it for today.' She reached for her seatbelt. 'Do you want me to drop you back at the hotel?'

'If you'll let me buy you dinner,' said Campbell on an impulse and when she froze with her seat belt halfway across her, he held up his hands in a gesture of innocence. 'Don't panic, I'm not planning to make a move on you! You made your feelings clear enough about that,' he told her. 'I was just thinking that you'd done enough cooking today, and I'm sick of eating in a restaurant on my own.'

Tilly hesitated. Far from panicking, she was perversely miffed that Campbell had made his lack of intentions so obvious. It didn't help that she was perfectly aware that it was her own fault. She *had* told him that she didn't want to get involved, so she shouldn't complain that he had taken her at her word.

She should be glad, in fact. Her heart couldn't take another break. It would just shatter and there would be nothing left of it at all. She didn't dare let her guard down, Tilly reminded herself. It would be so easy to let Campbell in, but how could he not hurt her? He might amuse himself for a while, but he wouldn't stay for ever, and why should he? Look at her—overweight and screwed up and stuck in her rut. What could she possibly have to offer him compared to an incredible new job and a beautiful ex-wife who clearly would only have to crook a perfectly manicured finger to have him back?

No, face reality, Tilly, her mind told her firmly. *Campbell is not for you.*

The trouble was that her body hadn't quite got the message.

Instead of listening to what her head was saying, her body was simmering with awareness of him. All Campbell had to do was turn and smile and every nerve she possessed seemed to suck in its breath.

Tilly couldn't take her eyes off his hands, his mouth. She couldn't stop remembering how lean and hard his body had felt, couldn't stop wondering what it would be like to unbutton his shirt, to run her hands over his powerful muscles, to press her lips to his skin. To forget about her poor, broken heart and let him bear her down on to a bed, a couch, the floor—*anywhere*— as long as he made love to her.

That was the point where Tilly had to stop herself. Wasn't it Campbell who had accused her of having a vivid imagination? It wasn't always a good thing, she decided, not when it left you with a thudding heart and a dry mouth and your insides roiling and writhing with desire.

And if she was like this during the day, what sort of state would she be in sitting across a table from him, where the lighting would be soft and intimate and she would only have to move her hand a matter of inches to be able to touch him?

No, the sensible thing would be to go home and put herself firmly out of temptation's way.

On the other hand, Tilly's body argued back, it would be nice to have a meal someone else had cooked, and it wasn't fair to leave him on his own every night. There was no point in being silly. It was just a meal with a friend. What could be the harm in that?

'Dinner would be nice,' she said firmly. 'Thanks.'

They arranged to meet a couple of hours later at a restaurant in the centre of Allerby. That gave Tilly enough time to jump in the shower and then work herself into a frenzy of doubt about what to wear.

She didn't want to look as if she were trying too hard, or as if she were expecting anything more than a friendly dinner, but it would be nice to show Campbell that she didn't always look a mess. She dressed for comfort when she was cooking, and her shoes were always practical and flat. It wasn't exactly a glamorous look. As for what she had worn on that Scottish hillside, Tilly didn't want to think about what she had looked like then!

In the end she settled on a clinging wrap-over top in a lovely deep violet with a swirly black skirt which looked good with her favourite shoes. They had perilously high heels with cutaway sides and peep toes and Tilly felt a million times better about herself the moment she put them on. Really, she ought to wear them the whole time, she decided, and to hell with teetering around the kitchen all day or throwing out her back.

Even the shoes couldn't stop her feeling nervous as the taxi stopped outside the restaurant. Tilly knew it was stupid, but her heart was thumping ridiculously and her entrails were fluttery.

'Please, please don't let me make a fool of myself,' she prayed as she paid off the taxi and turned for the entrance. The restaurant was reputed to be the best in Allerby and Tilly had been doubtful that they would get a table at such short notice, but she should have known a little thing like the restaurant being full wouldn't stand between Campbell and getting what he wanted.

Taking a deep breath, she pulled open the door. The *maître d'* glided towards her, but Tilly had already seen Campbell. He rose from the table at the sight of her, and their eyes met across the restaurant.

Campbell had showered and shaved and, in his beautifully cut suit, he looked lean and cool and more than a little ruthless. He looked devastating. Tilly's knees felt as if they were about to buckle, and she swallowed hard.

See? her mind was nagging. *I told you this was a bad idea. Now how are you going to resist him?*

She pushed the thought aside. This was just a friendly dinner. But her mouth was dry as, oblivious to the *maître d'*, to anything except the man waiting for her, she walked over to join Campbell.

'Hi,' she said. The queen of sparkling repartee that was her.

Campbell felt as if all the oxygen had been sucked out of his lungs at the sight of her walking towards him in a tight top and a skirt that skimmed her gorgeous curves and shoes so sexy they practically left scorch marks on the floor.

Without thinking, he reached out to touch her. He couldn't help himself. He had a hand at her waist and was drawing her towards him before the red alert siren went off belatedly in his head. He wasn't getting involved, right?

Right.

So yanking her into his arms and kissing her, pulling her towards him and exploring all that tantalising warmth and softness, making it his, right there in front of everybody, was probably *not* a good idea.

His senses screamed in protest as he regained control at the very last moment and dropped a chaste kiss on the corner of her mouth instead.

Just breathing in her perfume, feeling the softness of her skin, grazing the alluring curl of her lips was enough to make Campbell's head reel, and he had to jerk his head back before he did something really stupid.

He had to clear his throat before he could speak. 'You look wonderful,' he managed at last and winced inwardly at the croak in his voice. Whatever had happened to cool Campbell Sanderson, famed for his focus and control?

'Thanks,' said Tilly. 'You brush up nicely yourself.'

She was surprised at how ordinary her voice sounded. The brief brush of his lips had been like an electric jolt and she had to sit down before her legs gave way. Her face was throbbing where his mouth had touched her, her waist tingling where his hard hand had held her.

She picked up the menu with hands that weren't quite steady and made a show of reading it.

'Hungry?' Campbell asked.

'You know me, I'm always hungry.'

But she wasn't, not really. Tilly couldn't concentrate. The words wavered before her eyes, and it was impossible to focus on them when every sense was fixed on Campbell on the other side of the table. His lashes were lowered over the keen eyes as he read his own menu. His fingers were drumming absently on the cloth, and his mouth was set in the cool, quiet line that made her heart turn over whenever she looked at it.

Tilly was hardly aware of what she ordered. The wine waiter appeared as soon as the waitress had gone and tried to discuss wine with Campbell, who simply closed the wine list and handed it back. 'Whatever's good,' he said brusquely. 'And whatever you can find most quickly.'

'You'll probably get the most expensive wine in the restaurant,' Tilly warned him as the wine waiter, disappointed, took himself off.

Campbell shrugged. 'I'd rather pay for it than endure a lot of poncey talk about it.'

Olivier had been a wine buff. He had spent ages perusing the wine list before every meal, and Tilly couldn't help thinking that it would be a nice change to have a meal out that wasn't punctuated with exhaustive lectures on grapes and vineyards and bouquets and aromas.

The wine waiter took Campbell at his word and came back almost immediately with a bottle. Evidently deciding they weren't worth any flourishes, he opened the bottle, poured two glasses and left.

Tilly lifted her glass. 'Here's to you surviving your latest dangerous mission!'

'All those giggling girls?' Campbell's laugh was rueful. 'I'd rather do just about anything than face a gaggle like that again!'

'My hero!'

'You mock,' he said severely, although there was a hint of a smile about his mouth, 'but I'm not used to girls—or not twelve-year-old ones anyway.'

'You don't have a sister, then?'

'No, it was just me and my brother growing up. Girls were an alien species for a long time.'

'We're not *so* different, you know,' said Tilly. 'You'd learn that soon enough if you had a daughter.'

The smile vanished abruptly. 'God forbid!' he said, horrified at the thought. 'I wouldn't know where to start dealing with a girl.'

'Oh, I wouldn't worry. She would deal with you,' Tilly reassured him. 'She'd have you wrapped round her little finger in no time! It's always the same with you macho men. You're putty in the hands of a little girl.'

'It's just as well I never had any kids then,' said Campbell dryly.

'Did you ever think about having children when you were married?'

He shook his head. 'No, babies weren't part of Lisa's plan, and I've never even considered it. I don't think I would have been a good father.'

Tilly put down her glass with a frown. 'Why do you say that?'

'I'm afraid I would have turned out like my own father.' He straightened his cutlery without looking at her. 'I suppose he loved us in his own way, but I never remember having fun with him, or doing the stuff other boys do with their fathers.'

'That's a shame,' said Tilly, remembering how her stepfather had been with Harry and Seb. 'He missed out on a lot.'

'We all did. I know you think I'm bad at expressing emotion, but you should have met my father. He was an army officer, a very moral man in lots of ways, but he had rigid standards that my brother and I never met. We used to try and outdo each other in a bid to please him but nothing we did was ever quite good enough. It didn't matter how well we did, he never praised us. I think he thought it would spoil us or something.'

'What about your mother?'

'She died when I was nine.' Campbell sighed. 'To be absolutely honest, I don't remember her that well. Looking back, I wonder what kind of life she had, married to my father. I suspect that any spirit she may have had was crushed out of her early on. And after that we were packed off to boarding school, which sounds heartless, but we liked it more than being at home with our father.'

Poor little boys, Tilly thought, her heart twisting with pity. She had seen what losing their mother had done to her own brothers at not much older than Campbell had been. At least she had been there for them, but Campbell had had no such softening influence against his joyless, demanding father.

'I see now why you're so competitive,' she said, as lightly as she could, and he gave her a crooked grin.

'My brother is a barrister now. He's worse than me!'

'Your father must have been proud of you both, even if he didn't show it. You've both been very successful.'

Campbell shrugged. 'He died when I was in the Marines. Since trying to please him hadn't got me anywhere, I'd started to rebel and I was heading off the rails. I was lucky the Marines took me,' he confessed. 'God knows where I would have ended up otherwise, but I was too much of a maverick to make a successful career in the forces like my father did. I'm not sure even that would have been enough for Dad.' His mouth twisted in self-mockery. 'Lisa used to tell me I was still trying to prove myself to him.'

You didn't need to be married to him to guess that, Tilly thought waspishly. She wasn't going to give Lisa any points for insight.

Absently, she crumbled a piece of bread, imagining Campbell as a boy, growing into a wild young man, his mother dead, his father distant, driven always by the need to succeed. No wonder he wasn't good at talking about emotions. Being abandoned by his wife wouldn't have helped either. Underneath that surface cool, was he as lost as the rest of them?

Her heart cracked for him, but she knew better than to offer pity.

'My father is disappointed in me, too,' she offered. 'He doesn't think making cakes is a proper job. It doesn't make enough money, and that's his only measure of success.'

Campbell wasn't sorry to change the subject. 'Have you seen him since your mother died?'

'We keep in touch,' said Tilly. 'We have lunch every now and then, but it's never very successful. I think it's because we're so different, but *he* thinks it's because I've never forgiven him for leaving Mum. There may be some truth in that, although I know Mum was much happier with Jack than she would have been if Dad had stayed with us.'

'How old were you when your parents divorced?'

'Nearly seven,' she said. 'My mother kept telling me that my father still loved me, and that his leaving was nothing to do with me, but I didn't believe her. If he'd loved me, he wouldn't have left.'

She stopped and cocked her head, as if listening to what she had just said. 'Hmm, that sounds bitter, doesn't it? Maybe Dad's right after all!'

Campbell wasn't fooled by her bright smile. 'You stayed with your mother, then?'

'Yes, I had occasional weekends with Dad, but he was always busy. He got married again, and his new wife went perfectly with the smart, super-successful life he'd always wanted. Unfortunately a tubby little girl who reminded him of his old life just didn't blend with his décor!

'It was always a relief to go home,' Tilly remembered. 'I loved Jack. He was calm and steady and safe, and I was so happy when my mother married him. Once the twins arrived, it felt like the perfect family.'

She smiled wistfully. 'I suppose I always hoped that I would meet someone like Jack myself. Instead, as Cleo is always pointing out, I seem drawn to men like Olivier, who are much more like my father. That's all going to stop, though.' She put on a resolute air. 'From now on, I'm only interested in nice, kind men.'

Well, that ruled him out, Campbell thought. No one would ever describe him as nice or kind. It was on the tip of his tongue to tell Tilly that she was much too exciting to be content with merely nice and that she would be bored rigid after a week, but he stopped himself just in time.

It wasn't his business. He was leaving.

Focus on the new job, he told himself. Focus on Lisa and what it's going to be like seeing her again. But all he could think about was Tilly—warm, desirable, messy Tilly, with the candlelight glowing in her dark blue eyes and the mouth that made his mind go blank.

Campbell had never met a woman so easy to talk to. He liked her spiky, self-deprecating wit and the animation in her face. He liked the smile that lit her up from inside, the glint in her eyes as she teased him. She was never still. She fiddled with the wax dribbling down the candles, or traced invisible patterns on the cloth with her glass. She sat back, and leant forward, folding her arms on the table and just about giving Campbell a heart attack as her cleavage deepened.

'Let's get you a taxi,' he said gruffly when they at last came to leave. Not trusting himself to touch her, he shoved his hands deep into his pockets and walked beside her to the taxi rank in silence.

At least they didn't have to wait. Campbell wasn't at all sure what that would have done to his self-control. He should have gone with Tilly to see her home himself, but there was no way he could manage sitting in the back seat in the dark without reaching for her.

He leant through the window of the taxi at the head of the rank and handed the driver a note that would more than cover Tilly's fare. 'Make sure she gets safely in,' he said as the driver pocketed it quickly, unable to believe his luck.

'There's no need for that,' Tilly protested. 'I can get my own taxi.'

'I know you can, but I'm getting this one.'

Tilly opened her mouth to argue, then shut it again. Campbell's jaw was set at an angle that suggested she could argue all night and it still wouldn't make any difference.

'Well…thank you,' she said awkwardly instead. 'And thank you for dinner. It was lovely.' At least she assumed it had been. Too fixated on trying to keep her gaze from crawling all over Campbell, she could barely remember what she had eaten. Never had she paid less attention to food.

'I'll see you soon then.' Campbell's voice was brisk, but when their eyes met, the air shortened alarmingly between them.

'Yes,' she managed on a gasp.

'Goodnight, Tilly,' he said.

'Goodnight.'

Tilly's heart was pounding and her legs felt as if they were about to buckle. She badly needed to sit down. *Get in the car*, her mind screamed at her. *Get in the car—now! You'll regret it if you don't, you know you will.*

So it wasn't as if she didn't know what she should do, but somehow Tilly couldn't move. She couldn't even drag her eyes from his, so there was no way later she could claim that she had been caught unawares, as her mind was pointing out in no uncertain terms. *This is* so *not a good idea*, her mind scolded, but it was too late to back away now and, anyway, Tilly didn't want to. Her mind might be backing away and moaning *no, no, no*, but her body was screaming *yes, yes, yes!*

And her body won.

As if in slow motion, she saw Campbell lower his head towards her, and then his mouth captured hers and sensations Tilly hadn't even known existed exploded inside her. She parted her lips on a gasp that was part thrill, part alarm at the dizzying loss of control as she felt herself submerge beneath a rush of response. Every cell in her body was clamouring to press closer, taste more, touch again and again and again…

Her arms went round his waist and she leant into him, giddy with the feel of him. His lips were warm and sure as they explored her mouth, his tongue teasing, his hands hard and insistent. He smelt wonderful, tasted better, and she clung to him almost feverishly. He was her solid anchor, her safe harbour, the one point of certainty in a world that was unravelling with electrifying speed, and she kissed him back, oblivious to the waiting taxi, oblivious to anything except the gathering need and the deep, dark pulse of desire inside her.

And then, abruptly, it was over.

Campbell stepped back and opened the taxi door. His jaw was set and a muscle jerked in his cheek, but Tilly was too dazed to take much else in. Somehow she got herself into the back seat of the taxi. Campbell closed the door without a word and the taxi drove off, leaving him standing on the pavement and cursing himself for a fool.

CHAPTER EIGHT

TILLY fumbled with the seat belt. Her body was raging with disappointment and frustration. Why had he stopped? She had no idea now of how long the kiss had lasted. Could it really have been just a brief goodnight kiss?

But then why would it mean any more to Campbell? Tilly asked herself disconsolately. He must have picked up on the vibes she had tried so hard to suppress all night, and realised that all she could think about was touching him. Maybe he had thought to himself, why not? Or, worse, had decided to indulge her.

Body still thumping, she scowled miserably out of the window. *I told you so*, her mind said smugly. *I knew you'd regret it.*

But she didn't, not really. She had had to know what it felt like to kiss him, to hold him. The trouble was that now that she did, she wanted it again, she wanted more. Tilly had never had much time for the saying that a taste of honey was worse than none at all, but it was starting to make more sense.

Perhaps she *could* have more. The daring thought slid into her mind and she sat up straighter, as if shocked at her own presumption.

If she made it clear to Campbell that she had no expectations of any relationship, if she could convince him that it would just be a physical thing as far as she was concerned, would he be prepared to kiss her again? To make love to her? To share a night where they could shrug off the past and the future, where they could put aside hopes and fears, and not think at all, where nothing would matter but touching and tasting and feeling and the heady swell of pleasure?

Tilly's mouth was dry, her heart hammering at the mere thought of it. A single night… Would it be worth it? *Yes,* her body shouted. *Yes, yes, yes!*

What about your poor heart? her mind countered immediately, the way Tilly had known it would. *What if Campbell breaks it?*

She wouldn't let him break it, Tilly decided firmly. She would keep her heart intact. There would be no question of loving him. It would just be…sex.

She could suggest it, and see what Campbell said. She was a grown woman, he was a man. Surely they could talk about sex without embarrassment. He could only say no. It would be perfectly simple.

Or would it?

Tilly's confidence, ever fragile, faltered whenever she imagined facing Campbell with her proposition. *Campbell, about Friday night*, she could begin, but she couldn't decide what to say after that. *Could we try that again*, she might suggest, *but next time, don't stop and put me in a taxi.*

Perhaps it would be better to be more upfront. *I was wondering how you felt about a brief affair before you go?* Somehow Tilly couldn't see herself carrying that one off.

She couldn't decide whether she was glad or sorry that she wouldn't see him the next day. The arrangement had been that the participants in the competition would have the weekend off, presumably so that they could go home if necessary, but when Campbell had indicated that he wouldn't be going back to London it had seemed only polite to invite him for Sunday lunch.

Seb and Harry were coming home for the weekend on Saturday, and Tilly had been pleased at first. She had thought that her aching awareness of Campbell would be easier to handle if the boys were there to dilute the atmosphere, but now she wished they were staying at their respective universities and partying too hard the way they usually did. She loved Harry and Seb dearly, but she could hardly propose an affair in front of her younger brothers.

As it turned out, Seb and Harry were both still in bed nursing hangovers when Campbell arrived on Sunday. Having practised exactly what she would say if the opportunity arose, Tilly promptly forgot every word when she opened the door. The sight of him was like a fist thumping into her stomach, driving the breath from her lungs and leaving her reeling with a strange mixture of shock and delight.

Somehow she'd expected him to have changed since that kiss, but he looked exactly the same as always: cool, contained, faintly austere. It was hard to believe that only thirty-six hours ago he had held her hard against him and kissed her, that the stern mouth had been warm and sure and exciting on hers.

Campbell's expression gave nothing away. The pale, piercing eyes were guarded, Tilly thought, and her entrails churned. It was all very well deciding to be cool and upfront, but it all seemed a lot harder when you were faced with six feet of solid, detached male.

Flustered, she led the way to the kitchen and explained about Seb and Harry in far too much detail.

'They should be down any minute now. Would you like a coffee while we're waiting?'

'No, thanks. I'm fine.'

He might be fine, but she needed something to do to distract herself from the memory of that kiss that reverberated in the air between them. Tilly busied herself checking the meat, and tried to ignore the silence yawning around them.

This was ridiculous, she told herself, exasperated. She was being pathetic. It was just Campbell, for heaven's sake. She had been able to talk to him perfectly easily before, so she should be able to now. Taking off the oven gloves, she turned from the oven with a deep breath.

'About Friday night,' she began, exactly as she had planned. She even sounded calm, which was quite something given that her nerves were jumping and jittering and jangling in a way that that made it hard to think, let alone string a coherent sentence together.

She didn't get a chance to say any more. Campbell held up a hand to stop her.

'It's OK,' he said. 'You don't need to say any more.'

'Er…I don't?'

'I need to apologise,' he said stiffly. 'I was out of order on Friday night. I didn't mean to kiss you, I was just…I wasn't thinking,' he confessed. 'All I can say is that I'm sorry, and that it won't happen again. I'll keep my hands to myself in the future.'

Ah.

How was she supposed to respond to that? Tilly wondered. Clearly Campbell regretted the kiss and had no intention of repeating it, so she could hardly force herself upon him now. Her heart twisted at the realisation, but the only thing to do was put a good face on it.

At least it wouldn't be difficult. She had years of experience of being 'good old Tilly' who could be relied upon to dispel any potential awkwardness with a smiling face.

'It must have been that wine,' she said lightly. 'I don't think either of us was thinking clearly on Friday evening. That'll teach you to leave the choice up to the wine waiter!'

There was no mistaking the relief in Campbell's expression. He had obviously been dreading a scene, or that she might do exactly what she had been planning to do and throw herself at him.

'It's good of you to take it like that,' he said. 'I'd be sorry if I had spoiled things between us.'

'There's no question of that,' said Tilly, keeping her bright smile firmly in place.

'I was afraid I might have jeopardised our chances on the programme.'

Of course, the programme. Tilly had almost forgotten about that. It was telling that Campbell hadn't. He might be momentarily distracted by a kiss, but he would never lose sight of his ultimate goal.

'The only thing that will really jeopardise them is if you can't make Cleo's cake,' she told him and he grimaced.

'I know. It's harder than I expected,' he admitted.

Convincing herself that it was all for the best was harder than Tilly had expected, too. No matter how fiercely she reminded herself that he was leaving soon, or that he was still hung up on his ex-wife, disappointment still twisted painfully inside her. She made herself remember how much it had hurt when Olivier had gone, of how much better off on her own she would be in the long run, but none of it helped.

There was nothing to be done but keep the smile on her face, but it was feeling fixed by the time first Seb and then Harry appeared, yawning and rubbing their rumpled hair. In spite of their hangovers, they brightened considerably at Tilly's suggestion that they take Campbell to the pub while she finished getting lunch ready.

Campbell was all set to demur. 'We can't leave you alone to do all the work,' he protested.

'Honestly, it's better if we do,' Seb confided, and Harry

nodded vigorous agreement. 'She'll just get ratty if we hang around.'

'We could help,' Campbell suggested, but they only looked at him as if he had sprouted a second head.

Tilly rolled her eyes. 'Their idea of "helping" was to send me off for a weekend in the Highlands and look where that got me! No, you go,' she told him. 'Seb's right, you'll all just get in the way. There's not much more to do, in any case.'

She was desperate to get rid of them and have a few minutes to herself so that she could stop putting on a front.

Seeing that she was serious, Campbell let himself be persuaded, and the three men walked down to the local pub together. Tilly's brothers were very young but engaging company, and they were obviously very fond of their sister.

Over a beer, they told him all about Olivier. 'What a tosser!' said Harry dismissively. 'I'm glad Tilly isn't with him any more, but she was really cut up about him. She deserves better.'

Seb nodded. 'I mean, we give her a hard time, of course, but she's done everything for us. She stayed in Allerby and worked so that we could have a home and now we've gone we think it's time she got out and had a life for herself. That's why we put her up for this television thing. We thought it would be good for her. Left to herself, she'd just stay stuck in her kitchen and the truth is we don't like to think of her being on her own.'

'No,' his twin chimed in. 'Tilly needs someone to love, and she's not going to find anyone if she doesn't go out and look. The trouble is, she's got lousy taste. Knowing her, she'll just end up with another loser like Olivier!'

That made Campbell feel even worse about kissing her the other night. He had acted purely on instinct, and he had been taken aback by how sweet she had tasted, how good it had felt to hold her in his arms—how *right* it had seemed.

It had been a huge effort to make himself stop but, if he

hadn't, there was only one way it could have ended. Rather late in the day, Campbell had remembered how honest Tilly had been about not wanting to get involved. She had been badly hurt, he had *known* that, and she deserved better than a Friday night fumble.

He should have had more control, Campbell blamed himself austerely. He didn't like to think about how thoughtless he had been. It wasn't like him to lose sight of what was what. Perhaps Tilly was right, and the wine was to blame?

Whatever the reason, he had felt stupidly nervous about seeing her again today. He'd been afraid that she would have been embarrassed about the kiss, and awkward about telling him that she didn't want a repetition—as she clearly didn't. At least he had got in first with his apology to save her having to find the words. It had seemed the least he could do.

It was all sorted, anyway. He had taken evasive measures, a potentially difficult situation had been resolved, and all he had to do now was make that damn wedding cake. Then he could leave to get on with the rest of his life. It was the right thing to do for both of them.

So why didn't it feel right?

Campbell's video diary:
[Clears throat] I've been reminded to record this tonight, as there's only one more day to go. Tomorrow I've got to make Cleo's wedding cake, assemble it, decorate it and get it to the hotel in time for the party in the evening. I've planned much more difficult missions in my time, but I've got to admit this is the one I feel most nervous about. Cleo wants lemon sponge cake, so it has to be made fresh, and that means I don't get a trial run. But I'm sure it will be fine. I've been practising. Tilly has showed me how to cut the cake into blocks and then assemble them in the right

shape, and I've learnt how to ice and use a piping bag—which I have to say I never thought I would hear myself say! Tilly is a good teacher. Very good, in fact.

There's much more to the cake-making business than I realised. I've seen how Tilly makes a real connection with people, not just when it comes to the design and what's likely to be suitable, but when she's delivering the cakes. [Relaxing as forgets camera and pursues own thoughts] I think her brothers may be wrong about her being stuck in the kitchen. It seems to me that Tilly is out all the time and that she knows a lot of people.

Yesterday, for instance, we went to the hospice she'll donate her cheque to if we win. It was quite an experience. I'd never been anywhere like it before. I expected it to be a depressing place, to be honest, but it wasn't. It felt bright and light and peaceful and I felt... [Pause, searching for the right word] ...well, I suppose I was moved. Yes, moved.

Tilly was quite at ease there. She seemed to know everyone, but she told me afterwards that she didn't. I think people respond to her warmth. There's a kind of brightness about her ...[Abruptly recollects camera] Anyway...well, I can see how much winning would mean to the hospice, so I'd better make Cleo a good cake tomorrow and make sure we get the maximum number of points.

I can't see why we shouldn't. I've done a bit of research and got a picture of an ancient Egyptian barge and the costumes and so on. I even had a look at the play. Tilly drew up a design and kept it as simple as possible, but it's still going to be tricky. I'll be glad when tomorrow's over.

[Stops, realises that hasn't sounded very sure] Yes, of

course I will be. I need to get back to work. I've got things to do. I want the cake to be a success tomorrow, but then it will be time to say goodbye.

Tilly's video diary:
[Pushes hair tiredly from face] I can't believe it's almost over. Campbell has just gone back to his hotel for the last time. He'll be back tomorrow to make Cleo's cake, but then he's leaving. It's funny to think how much has changed since the last time I recorded this diary. Campbell's changed—or maybe it's just that I've got to know him better. Or maybe I'm the one that's changed.

The kitchen won't be the same without him. I mean, he can be really irritating. He insists in clearing up immaculately—and I mean immaculately—*every five minutes, which I know is a good thing, and I should do that, too, but sometimes when you're doing a tricky bit of piping you don't want someone asking, 'Have you finished with the sugar because I'll put it away if you have?' or, 'If you just stand away from the table a minute, I'll wipe up the extraordinary mess you've created'. The worst thing is, I think I'm going to miss it. [Sighs]*

Anyway…he's learnt how to make a sponge. The thing about Campbell is that he's really focused. If he decides he's going to do something, he'll do it. He'd never admit it, but I think he might be a bit nervous about Cleo's cake. It's a difficult design. Too difficult for a beginner, but he's determined to get it right. I hope he does. I'm not supposed to have anything to do with it, but I'll be around to give advice until I have to go to the wedding ceremony at three. There's a small reception afterwards, but the cake is for the party in the evening, so I'll come back after that and hopefully the cake will be all ready to go.

And then that'll be it. It's going to be…strange. But of course, Campbell has got his new job to go to, and I've got a business to run. [Stops, swallows] It'll be for the best, I know, but I hate saying goodbye.

'You won't forget the asp, will you?' It was the morning of Cleo's wedding, and Tilly was supposed to be getting ready for the ceremony, but she kept popping down to the kitchen where Campbell was making cakes with military precision.

'Stop flapping,' he said, exasperated. 'I'm the one that's supposed to be nervous here! It's all under control. Look!' He waved the time plan he had plotted minute by minute at her and checked his watch. 'Right now cakes five and six are supposed to be in the oven, and there they are, see,' he said, pointing at the oven. 'I'm going to take them out at thirteen ten.'

'I don't like all this precision,' Tilly fretted. 'This isn't a mission that can be planned down to the last second. The cakes will be ready when they're ready. Remember what I told you about the skewer? Keep an eye on them rather than the clock, that's all I'd say.'

Campbell wished she would go away. Quite apart from the fact that she was casting doubt on his plan, of which he was secretly very proud, she was far too distracting standing there in a faded towelling robe, with her hair wrapped up in a towel and her face clean and rosy from the shower.

She smelt of baby powder. It was all too easy to imagine pulling her towards him by the belt of her robe, shutting her up with a kiss while he untied it in one easy move so that he could slide his hands beneath the material to explore her lush body. She would be warm and sweet and clean.

Snarled up with longing and frustration, Campbell wished she wasn't standing between him and the sink. He could do with putting his head under the cold tap. As it was, he would have to pass her to do that, and he couldn't trust himself that close.

Ever since that kiss, he had been achingly aware of her. Again and again he had had to remind himself of all the reasons why he shouldn't touch her, but the reasons were sounding thinner with every day that passed.

He did his best to concentrate on the future, on the challenge of his new job and the move to New York but whenever he tried to imagine what it would be like, all he could picture was life without Tilly, quiet and cold and empty.

It was absurd. What was he thinking? Campbell demanded, exasperated with himself. That he should give up his career, his plans, the chance to turn round a company and make it a global leader again? Drop out of the race just before the finishing line? Of course he couldn't do that, and if he wouldn't contemplate any of that, it would hurt Tilly.

And that was something Campbell wasn't prepared to do.

'Shouldn't you be getting ready?' he asked her pointedly.

'Yes, I'd better go and dry my hair.' She looked anxious. 'Are you sure you're OK?'

'Everything's fine.'

If only it were, Campbell thought as she whisked out of the kitchen and he could let out a long, very careful, breath at last. Right then everything felt as if it might slip out of control any minute, and that wasn't a feeling he liked at all.

Squaring his shoulders, he turned his attention back to his time plan. Focus, that was all he needed to do. It had always worked for him in the past and in a lot more difficult situations than this. It would work now.

It was hard to focus, though, when Tilly reappeared at last, spilling out of a deep aqua-blue suit. A bag was wedged under her arm while she fastened her earrings.

'OK, I'm off,' she said, her face intent as she fiddled with the second stud.

Her outfit wasn't particularly daring. It had a cropped jacket, nipped in at the waist, and a lacy camisole gave modesty to the plunging neckline. A flippy skirt ended at the knee. Her shoes were precipitously heeled, true, with ridiculous bows. Otherwise, it was the kind of outfit you would expect a woman to wear to a wedding.

So there was no reason for Campbell to feel as if his head was reeling. He actually had to close his eyes.

'What's the matter?'

He snapped them open to find that Tilly had sorted out her earrings and was watching him. 'Nothing,' he said tightly. 'Nothing at all.'

She wasn't satisfied, but made matters worse by coming closer and peering at him. 'You look as if you're in pain.'

If only she knew! 'I'm fine.' Campbell managed a controlled smile. 'Just thinking about what needs to be done.'

Like take a cold shower.

'Well, if you're sure...' Tilly checked her bag. 'Now, you've got the design?'

'Yes, yes,' he said impatiently.

'And you haven't forgotten about piping the names on the side of the barge, the way we discussed? Make sure you spell them right, too. It's all noted on the design. Do you think I should check it quickly?'

'No,' said Campbell. 'I think you should go. You'll be late.'

Tilly looked at her watch and squeaked with dismay. 'God, yes, I will be...' Grabbing the keys to the van, she hurried to the door. 'I'll be back later,' she called on the way out of the room. 'Good luck!'

By the time she returned, Campbell had himself well under control. He just had to keep his hands to himself for a few more hours. He could do that. Look, he had even made a wedding cake, and if he could do that, he could do anything!

He had to admit that he was secretly very proud of the cake. It looked just like Tilly's sketch. Sitting on top of the cake base was the cake Cleopatra's cake barge, complete with a cake Antony, dressed as a Roman general, and even a cake asp, curled ironically in a corner. Authenticity had suffered with the tin cans trailing off the back and the large sign with 'just married' iced carefully on to it, but all in all it was pretty damn impressive, Campbell thought.

He could hardly believe that he had made it himself.

He was changed and ready to go as soon as Tilly got back. That was what you could do when you stuck to your time plan.

Tilly's face when she came into the kitchen and saw the finished cake was everything Campbell could have hoped for.

'Oh, Campbell, it's *fabulous*!' she cried. 'Well done! I know we talked about it but it's so different when you see it made up. Wait till Cleo sees it! She's going to be so thrilled,' she said as she walked round the table to inspect the cake more closely. 'This is bound to win!

'It's incredible to think that a fortnight ago you didn't even know how to make a basic sponge,' she told him admiringly. 'I'm so *proud* of you! This is going to be the highlight of the party tonight and—'

She stopped.

'What?' asked Campbell.

'The names on the side of the barge,' she said in a hollow voice.

'What about them?'

'You've spelt Anthony wrong.'

'I have not!' Campbell was outraged at the suggestion. 'I made a point of checking.'

'Not against my design.' Tilly snatched up the sketch-book and thrust it at him. 'How is Anthony spelt there?'

'With an "h".'

'Yes, and it's spelt with an "h" because that's how Anthony spells his name, so why have you spelt it without one?'

'Because that's the correct spelling,' said Campbell, sure of his ground. 'I even rang up a mate of mine who's a lecturer in English and specialises in sixteenth-century drama, and he told me Shakespeare's Antony definitely doesn't have an "h".'

'Maybe not, but Cleo's Anthony *does*,' said Tilly, exasperated.

Campbell was seriously put out. He had gone to a lot of trouble to make sure that everything was right. 'What was the point of finding out what Cleopatra's barge might have looked like and exactly what Antony would have been wearing, if you're not going to get his name right?' he demanded crossly.

'Because it's Tony and Cleo's wedding cake, not an academic treatise! Why do you have to be such a pedant? I know you like to be precise, but this is ridiculous! The whole point is that it's *their* names because it's *their* wedding!' She threw the sketch-book on to the table, furious with him for spoiling things when everything else looked so perfect. 'We're going to have to change it.'

Campbell was equally irritable. 'Who's going to notice?'

'Tony will, for a start. And his parents. Cleo says his mother is the queen of nit-pickers and is always moaning about missing apostrophes and the misuse of commas. She's the kind of person who sends back thank you letters with the spelling mistakes corrected! She's *bound* to comment. If there's one thing you ought to be able to get right at a wedding it's the groom's name, after all!'

A muscle was working furiously in Campbell's cheek. 'There isn't time to change it now,' he pointed out. 'It'll mean taking off all that icing.'

'There is if we do it together.' Tilly tossed an apron to him and tied on another over her wedding outfit.

The television cameras would be there again tonight. She didn't want them filming Cleo's new mother-in-law complaining that Campbell had made a mistake. She might be livid with him herself, but he had worked so hard on the cake and it looked fantastic. Trust him to mess everything up by insisting on being right!

Part of Tilly wanted to pick up the cake and crown him with it, but another part was already working out how to fix things. The cake had to be perfect for Cleo, and there was the competition to think of, too. Campbell might be the biggest nit-picker on the planet, but winning was important to him, and there was no way Tilly was going to let a little icing stand in the way when they were this close to victory.

'You make up some more yellow icing for the timbers,' she told him, 'and I'll do some white for the lettering. Then we just need to scrape off what's there, retouch it a bit and pipe on the new names.'

Campbell looked at his watch. 'We're supposed to be there in less than half an hour.'

'It takes ages for a party to get going.' Tilly was already shaking out icing sugar. 'Better for us to be a bit late than spend the whole evening being told we've spelt Anthony's name wrong! Come on, let's get going.'

Of course it took longer than expected, and in the end Tilly piped on the names as they couldn't afford to make the slightest mistake.

'We're cutting it very fine,' Campbell warned, anxious to make up for his blunder with the name. But how the hell was he supposed to have known that when Tilly had said spell a name correctly she had actually meant spell it wrong?

'We'll just have to hope there's not too much traffic. You drive,' Tilly said, tossing him the keys. 'You'll be faster than me. I'll hold the cake.'

They were in such a hurry by then that they didn't even stop to take off their aprons. Campbell took off with a squeal of brakes and drove with a nerveless skill that had Tilly clutching the cake box.

She didn't tell him to slow down, though. If they didn't get there before the television crew, she was sure they would lose points for being late, and she was determined now that they should win. It would be good to be able to give the money to the hospice, of course, but more than that she wanted to win because it mattered to Campbell.

The party was being held at a country house hotel some ten miles outside Allerby.

'We'll take the dual carriageway,' said Tilly as they screeched to a halt before yet another red light. 'We'll never get there if we have to stop at all these lights and get past all these stupid people dithering around looking for somewhere to park.'

She directed him out to the ring road, where at last Campbell could put his foot down. The pink van wasn't exactly powerful, but it responded valiantly, shuddering at the unfamiliar speed as they shot down the outside lane.

'It's not the next roundabout, but the next one,' said Tilly. 'We don't want to miss the turning. What is it?' she asked as Campbell glanced in the rear-view mirror and stamped on the brake, swearing under his breath.

'Police,' he said curtly.

'Please tell me you're joking!'

But Campbell had rarely felt less like joking and the next moment Tilly saw for herself as a policeman on a motorbike came alongside and flagged them, pointing over to the hard shoulder.

Campbell had little choice but to obey. He wound down his window as the officer approached.

'Would you get out of the car, please, sir?'

Rigid with frustration and temper, Campbell got out, remembering too late that he still had his pink apron on.

The policeman eyed him for a moment, and then read the side of the van. 'Let me guess,' he said. 'You're Mr Sweet, are you, sir? Or would that be Mr Nothing?'

Campbell set his teeth. 'Neither,' he said tersely, struggling to get rid of the apron so that he could dig in his back pocket for his wallet and driving licence. He couldn't have a sensible conversation wearing the stupid thing. This was all Tilly's fault for insisting that he wear one.

The policeman inspected the driving licence. 'Were you aware that you were exceeding the speed limit?'

'I can explain, officer. We've got something of an emergency.'

'This isn't the way to the hospital.'

'It's not that kind of emergency.' For a wild moment Campbell wondered whether he should pretend that Tilly was about to give birth, but presumably few mothers stopped to put on high heels and make-up when they went into labour. 'We've got this cake,' he began.

'Cake?' the policeman repeated expressionlessly.

'Yes. It's for a wedding.'

Campbell trailed off, realising how absurd it must sound but before he could say any more, Tilly had emerged from the van, having set the cake carefully on the seat. She had had the foresight to remove her apron, which gave the policeman a splendid view of her cleavage, Campbell noted.

'I'm afraid it's all my fault, officer.' Her eyes were huge and dark as she gazed limpidly at the policeman, who was clearly finding it difficult not to stare at the plunging neckline with its tantalising glimpse of lace below.

'It's my best friend's wedding,' she went on in a breathy voice that Campbell had never heard her use before, 'and I promised *faithfully* that I would have this cake ready for when she got to the party, but we had all sorts of problems, and now we're late and Cleo's going to be *so* disappointed, and it's her wedding day and I can't *bear* to think of letting her down so I was making Campbell drive fast...'

Campbell watched in reluctant admiration as words tumbled breathlessly from her, befuddling the policeman with their speed and intensity.

'It's really not his fault, officer. He wouldn't normally *dream* of speeding, and I know you're just doing your job and of course you must, but could we please, please, just get the cake to the wedding first and then we'll report to the police station or whatever you want.'

Taking the policeman's arm, she dragged him over to look through Campbell's open window. 'Look, you can see we're telling the truth. There's the cake, and it's so beautiful. Cleo will be devastated if we don't get it there in time, and we're already so late! I'll never forgive—'

Bemused by the flood of words, or possibly by the allure of Tilly's cleavage, the policeman backed away from the van. He had evidently given up trying to make sense of it all and simply held up a hand to stop Tilly in mid-sentence.

'Where is this wedding?' he asked gruffly.

'At Hammerby Hall. It's—'

'I know where it is.' He waved them back to the van. 'If I catch you speeding again, I won't be so lenient,' he warned them, 'but I'll make allowances for today. We don't want to disappoint the bride, do we?'

Climbing on to his bike, he kicked up the stand and switched on the flashing light. 'Follow me.'

CHAPTER NINE

CAMPBELL pulled out after the policeman, who was already speeding ahead along the dual carriageway, siren blaring, to clear the traffic out of their way, and for a good minute there was utter silence in the van.

Then they both started to laugh at the same time.

'I can't believe you got away with that!' said Campbell, still laughing but trying to sound disapproving. 'I've never seen such a revolting display! *I'm so sorry, officer,*' he mimicked her breathy voice. '*Please look down my cleavage instead of writing a speeding ticket.*'

Tilly wiped her eyes. 'It worked, didn't it? It's not as if you were getting far.' She burst into giggles again. 'I wish you could have seen your face when he asked if you were Mr Sweet!'

Campbell snorted and shook his head. 'That was your fault for making me wear that stupid apron!' he said but his attempt at disgust was short-lived in the face of Tilly's infectious laughter, and in the end he gave in and laughed too as they sped after the policeman.

Thanks to their escort, they arrived bare moments before the bridal party. Waving a grateful farewell to their policeman, Tilly and Campbell hurried in and were just lifting the cover off the cake when the television crew turned up, all ready to record Cleo's reaction.

She didn't disappoint, squealing with delight when she clapped eyes on the cake and throwing her arms around Campbell's neck.

'It's *so* fabulous! You clever thing!' she exclaimed as she planted a resounding kiss on his cheek. 'Thank you so much, Campbell. It's the best wedding cake ever! I'm never going to be able to cut it. Oh, I think I might be going to cry, it's so perfect.'

Alarmed at the prospect of tears, Campbell patted her gingerly and rolled his eyes over her shoulder at Tilly in a silent plea for help.

'Cleo, what do you think of Antony's costume?' she asked, coming to his rescue. 'Campbell researched it down to the last detail. He's even got the shoes right!'

To Campbell's relief, Cleo let go of him and bent to examine the cake in more detail. 'It's incredible. I can't believe you've learnt to do this in just two weeks, Campbell! Tony, come and look at this.'

Fortunately for Campbell, her groom restrained himself from hugging, but he was equally complimentary. 'This is really impressive,' he said to Campbell. 'I can see a hell of a lot of research has gone into it.' He walked round the cake, inspecting it closely. 'Isn't Cleopatra's Antony spelt without an "h", though?'

Tilly met Campbell's gaze across the cake. A definite smile was tugging at his mouth, and the sight of it unlocked something deep in her chest, releasing a disquieting tingle that seeped slowly along her veins.

'Could we have a quick interview?'

Suzy's voice at her elbow startled Tilly out of her thoughts. The producer drew her and Campbell away from the crowd gathering round the cake and beckoned Jim, the cameraman, over.

'It's certainly a wonderful cake, Campbell,' Suzy began. 'Is it really all your own work?'

'Yes,' said Tilly, as Campbell said, 'No.'

Suzy looked from one to the other.

'I had to have Tilly's help in the end,' he told her. 'I'd made a mistake, and Tilly put it right.'

'Why did you say that?' Tilly demanded crossly under her breath while Suzy was conferring with the cameraman. 'Now we'll lose points! I thought you wanted to win.'

'I do, but I'm not going to cheat to do it. The rules were clear. I had to make the cake entirely myself.'

'You did that! It was perfect.'

'It wasn't perfect. I spelt the name wrong, and you had to put it right.'

Tilly chewed her lip. 'No one would ever have known it wasn't you. You'd done it exactly the same, just without the "h".'

'I would have known,' said Campbell. He looked at her curiously. 'You've changed your tune, haven't you? I thought you didn't care whether we won or not?'

Tilly couldn't meet his eyes. She couldn't tell him that she only wanted to win for his sake. 'We've gone to all this effort,' she said. 'It just seems a shame to blow it now.'

'We've done what we can,' he said carelessly. 'It's down to the viewers now. One way or another, it'll be over soon.'

Tilly looked away. Yes, it would all be over soon, and that was probably just as well. The tension over the last few days had been almost unendurable, erupting at last in that stupid row over how to spell Anthony. She had been torn between not wanting their time together to end and wishing that it would so that she wouldn't have to live any longer with the breathless churning that gripped her whenever she looked at Campbell.

She was going to miss him so much, but there would be a certain relief in not having to fight the attraction any more. She had to think about that, and not about how empty the kitchen was going to be without his solid, straight but somehow steadying presence. She couldn't allow herself to think about how the severe expression relaxed when he was amused, crinkling the corners of his eyes and deepening the creases on either side of his mouth.

His mouth...she definitely couldn't afford to let herself think about that. *Or* his hands. Or the whole lean, muscled length of him.

It was extraordinary how a man so austere and restrained-looking on the surface could have reduced her to a state of feverish desire where the most casual brush against each other left her boneless, a smile would stop the breath in her throat and the touch of his hand was like a jolt of electricity.

Campbell wasn't romantic, he wasn't passionate, he wasn't any of the things Tilly yearned for in a man. He was tough and terse and acerbic, and she wanted him in a way she had never wanted anyone before.

But she couldn't have him. He was leaving. Remember that, Tilly?

She wished now that she had ignored his reluctance and told him how she felt after that kiss. At least they could have had a week together and she would have had some memories. But it was too late now. Tomorrow he would be gone.

There was no point being miserable about it, Tilly decided, forcing her shoulders back and fixing on a bright smile. She had made a choice and now she had to live with it. In the meantime, it was Cleo's wedding, and Cleo would want her to enjoy herself.

She threw herself into the party spirit with a touch of desperation, and it wasn't, after all, that hard. She knew lots of people and there was a very happy atmosphere, especially after Cleo and Tony performed a dance routine for all their guests. This seemed to involve Cleo pushing Tony around the floor and hissing exasperated instructions at him. Clearly, he didn't have a clue what he was supposed to be doing, and their audience was soon laughing uproariously.

Campbell looked at Tilly beside him. She was almost doubled over, helpless with laughter. Her face was alight, her eyes glowing, and he was seized by the urge to touch her, to hold her, to draw her warmth and her light around him.

So strong was the impulse that he had to make himself move away, but the more he tried to concentrate on making conversation with the other guests, the more aware he was of Tilly, scintillating, sparkling, in the background. She was talking and laughing, smiling, hugging friends, kissing acquaintances on the cheeks, and Campbell was gradually consumed by the longing to stride over, take hold of her and pull her away, outside.

To make her smile at him. Touch *him*. Kiss *him*.

By the time Tilly danced over to him at last, he was in no state to be sensible. He couldn't remember why resisting her had ever seemed like an option, let alone a necessity, and every stern resolution evaporated as she stopped in front of him. Buoyed up by champagne and the party atmosphere, she was attempting to belly dance but succeeding only in looking faintly ridiculous and yet incredibly sexy at the same time.

'Come on, Campbell,' she cried over the throb of the music. 'Show us what you're made of!'

And Campbell gave in to the terrible temptation that had been tormenting him all evening and took her by the waist.

'How can I refuse an invitation like that?'

At the touch of his hands, Tilly abruptly lost her rhythm. She stumbled and would have fallen if he hadn't been holding her and instinctively she put her hands on his arms to balance herself.

And then she was lost.

The feverish gaiety that had swept her through the evening evaporated without warning, sucked away with the music and the laughter and the other guests behind some invisible barrier where everything was muted, leaving the two of them stranded and alone, while the space shrank around them, shortening the air and making her heart boom and thump and thunder in her ears.

It felt as if an insistent hand in the small of her back was pushing her towards Campbell, and it was a relief to give in, to let herself lean against him with a tiny sigh, knowing there was nothing else that she could do, that there was something more powerful than either of them forcing them together, insisting on balancing his hard strength and solidity with her softness and her warmth.

And, once she *had* given in, it felt so wonderful that Tilly wondered why she had ever believed that she ought to resist.

Afterwards, she could remember nothing about the music they danced to that evening. She knew only that she was holding Campbell at last, that he was holding her, and that they were dancing together.

Her arms slid up to his shoulders, savouring the feel of the powerful muscles beneath his jacket. Her face was almost touching his throat. She could see the pulse beating below his ear, and she breathed in the scent of clean skin and clean shirt and something that was purely Campbell.

Close to him, she felt light and shimmery, lit by the glow spreading through her, a glow that was burning brighter and brighter the tighter he held her. They were barely dancing, barely swaying, but his lips were against her hair, drifting downwards, and Tilly's mouth curved expectantly. They would reach her cheek soon. They would graze her jaw, would nuzzle the lobe of her ear until she gasped and arched, and then she would turn her head and they would kiss, and that glow would ignite into a flame, a *fire*…

Adrift in anticipation, Tilly didn't realise that the music had stopped until Campbell straightened slowly. His hands fell from her, but he held her still with his eyes, eyes that could look deep inside her and could surely see the desire beating there.

'Shall we go?' he asked, his voice deep and low, and Tilly nodded.

Still snared in the magic of the dance, she sat wordlessly beside Campbell as he drove the van back to the house. It seemed a long time since they had driven in the other direction, laughing helplessly as they'd followed their police escort.

Campbell was silent, too. They hadn't spoken at all, as if something stronger than both of them had them in its grip, but perhaps she had it wrong? The headlights from passing cars swept over them, illuminating the austere profile, and Tilly's stomach hollowed.

It won't happen again, he had told her after that one devastating kiss, and she knew instinctively that he would keep that promise. If she wanted him, it would be up to her to tell him that. Did she dare?

Careful, her heart reminded her. *Remember how much it hurt last time. You don't have to do this if you don't want to.* The choice was hers.

But with every sense, every cell in her body, clamouring for his touch, it didn't feel like much of a choice to Tilly. She had gone too far to turn back now. The best she could do was protect herself as best she could.

Just one night… What harm could there be in that? Her heart was on guard, so if she could just keep her emotions in check and make it clear to Campbell that she wasn't looking for anything more than a night together, surely that wouldn't be risking too much?

Campbell turned into her drive and parked outside the front door. He cut the lights and turned off the engine, plunging them into darkness and utter silence. For a moment, they both sat completely still, staring straight ahead through the windscreen.

It was up to her, Tilly remembered.

She moistened her lips. 'Do you remember being on that mountain?' she asked. She wanted to sound cool, but of course her voice came out thready and wavering.

'Ben Nuarrh?' Campbell turned to look at her, his expression impossible to read in the darkness, but she thought she detected an undercurrent of amusement. 'How could I forget?'

'Do…you remember how we talked about fantasies?' Tilly made herself persevere.

'Yes,' he said cautiously.

She took a deep breath. 'I've got a fantasy now.'

'Does it involve food?'

That was definitely a smile in his voice. Tilly wasn't sure whether that was an encouraging sign or not.

'Not this time.' She hesitated. 'It involves you.'

Campbell stilled, and this time when he spoke the laughter had vanished. 'Tell me.'

And, suddenly, it was easy after all.

'Well, in my fantasy we're here, like we are now, in the dark, but there's no future, no plans, no responsibilities, no being sensible. There's just the two of us and one night together.'

She swallowed. 'In my fantasy, you reach out and lay your palm against my cheek,' she said, and Campbell lifted his arm slowly and caressed her face.

The warmth of his hand made Tilly suck in a breath. 'You tell me that you're leaving tomorrow, but you want to spend tonight with me.'

'I want to spend tonight with you.' His voice was so low, it seemed to reverberate down her spine. 'I haven't been able to think about anything else for weeks now.'

'Hey, this is my fantasy,' said Tilly shakily. 'No improvising.'

'Sorry.' Even in the dim light she could see the quiver at the corner of his mouth, and she felt her bones liquefy.

'Then you tell me you haven't been able to think about anything else for weeks now.'

The quiver deepened. 'Then what?'

'Then...then you kiss me.'

There was a pause, then Campbell let his hand drift down to her throat, where it curved beneath her silky hair so that he could pull her with a breathless lack of speed towards him. Very, very slowly, he bent his head until their mouths met.

'Like this?' he murmured.

His lips were gentle at first, tantalising and persuasive, until Tilly leant into him with a tiny sigh as she parted her own and wound her arms around his neck to pull him closer.

It was so delicious to be able to kiss him, to taste him, to feel his hand at her knee, sliding insistently under her skirt as they kissed and kissed and kissed again—deep, sweet kisses that grew harder and hungrier with every moment.

'Yes, like that,' she said unsteadily, tipping back her head as Campbell's lips trailed down her throat, and his free hand flicked open the buttons on her jacket. 'Exactly like that.'

She gasped as she felt him smile against her skin, and his fingers tightened possessively on her thigh.

Kissing his way lazily back up to her earlobe, Campbell let his hands continue their delicious exploration. 'Do I get to tell you my fantasy yet?' he whispered in her ear and it was Tilly's turn to smile.

'What's yours?'

'You beg me to take you inside, right now, and make love to you all night.'

'I'm not sure I like the idea of begging,' Tilly managed and a laugh shook his big frame.

'It's my fantasy now,' he pointed out. 'Fair's fair.'

'How about if I ask nicely instead?'

'How nicely?'

She laughed, intoxicated with his touch. 'Very nicely,' she said. 'I'll ask very, very nicely.'

Pushing him back into his seat, she clambered into his lap so that she was straddling him, and took his face between her palms, covering it with teasing kisses, tickling him with her tongue.

'Please,' she whispered, kissing her way down his throat in her turn. 'Please, Campbell. Please take me to bed and make love to me all night.'

'That's *quite* nice,' said Campbell in a ragged voice. 'Ask me again.'

He was pushing aside her jacket, tugging up her silk camisole, and Tilly shuddered and writhed with pleasure as his hands closed on her bare skin.

'Please,' she gasped again. 'You don't need to pretend anything. It's not about love. It's not about forever. It's just you and me and one night together. Make love to me, please.'

'Well, since you asked so nicely…'

Somehow they got out of the van, but they couldn't bear to let go of each other, couldn't bear to stop kissing. For long, mindless minutes, Campbell pressed her against the driver's door and Tilly didn't care that the handle was digging into her hip, cared only that she could hold him and touch him and kiss him back.

At last they made it to the front door. There was a short delay while Tilly fumbled for keys, distracted by Campbell kissing her shoulder and the nape of her neck, as his hot, hungry hands explored beneath her open jacket. Her fingers shook as she inserted the key impatiently and they practically fell through the door, still kissing.

Unheeded, Tilly's bag fell to the floor, closely followed by the jacket Campbell was peeling from her shoulders. He pushed her back against the door and she arched beneath his touch, gasping his name as she clutched her fingers in his hair, incoherent with desire.

'What happens in your fantasy now?' Tilly asked shakily when he raised his head at last, and Campbell took her by the hand and tugged her towards her bedroom.

'I'll show you.'

Tilly mumbled and brushed at something on her face before rolling over to bury her face in a pillow.

'Wake up, Jenkins. It's breakfast time.' Campbell's voice, warm and threaded with laughter, slowly penetrated her sleep and she stirred, opening sleep-clouded eyes to find him sitting on the edge of the bed, tickling her cheek with a finger.

He smiled at her. 'I thought I'd make your fantasy come true.'

Tilly pulled herself blearily up on to the pillows. She felt boneless with pleasure still, as if she had been drenched in honeyed delight, and the colour rose in her cheeks as the memories of the night before flooded back.

'I think you've already done that,' she said, and he smiled.

'This is a different fantasy. You told me all about it on Ben Nuarrh. Don't you remember? You wanted to wake up with coffee and croissants.'

Brought by a gorgeous lover. Tilly did remember, and the fact that he did, too, made her heart turn over.

'Look,' said Campbell as he laid the tray on the bed. 'The sun's even shining.'

There was a ridiculous lump in her throat. Tilly swallowed. 'So it is.' Leaning forward, she made a big deal of breathing in the smell of coffee. 'Mmm,' she murmured appreciatively and unfolded a tea towel to find the promised croissants. They were even warm.

She lifted her eyes to his green ones and wondered how she could ever have thought of them as cold.

'Where did you find these?'

'At the shop on the corner. You were dead to the world so I thought it would be worth a trip.' He nodded down at the tray. 'I realise the orange juice wasn't specified in your fantasy. That's my own innovation.'

Tilly was overwhelmed. Nobody had ever done anything like this for her before.

Last night, he had made her feel beautiful and desirable; this morning, instead of being desperate to leave, as she had half expected, he had gone to all this trouble to make her a special breakfast. He had *remembered* something she had once said and acted on it to make her feel special.

He made her feel loved.

If you were talking fantasies, this one was hard to beat.

'Hey, stop that!' she said, deciding that her only option was to make a joke of it. It was that or cry. 'It's not fair to start being thoughtful and perfect now you're about to go!'

'You could come with me.'

'What, to the States?' she asked, keeping the smile fixed on her face and assuming that he was joking as well.

'Why not?'

Her smile faded as they looked at each other. He couldn't mean it.

Tilly didn't want to think that making love had been a mistake, but she was afraid that it probably had been. Now she was going to have to live with the memory of the heart-stopping rapture, of the consuming pleasure and the heady delight of touching and being touched, of the fierceness of the passion they had discovered together. Night after night, she would have to lie in this bed and remember and know that she would never feel that again. She would never hold him again, never kiss him again.

She would have to say goodbye and it would hurt.

She was a fool, in fact, but Tilly couldn't regret it. Just one night, they had agreed, and what a night it had been.

And now Campbell was suggesting—seriously?—that she wouldn't need to say goodbye after all.

There was no point in denying that she was tempted, but deep down Tilly knew this was just another fantasy. Maybe fantasies could come true for a night, even for a morning, but how could they endure day after day, in the harsh realities of life?

She couldn't go to the States with Campbell. Her business was here, her friends were here. And what would he do with her over there? He was a high-powered businessman, she was a homely cake-maker. Their lives would barely coincide. Tilly had seen what different aspirations had done to her parents' marriage.

No, she had ignored her sensible side long enough. This was no time to believe in fantasies. It could never work. Campbell was driven by the need to win. His priorities were different, his life was different.

And he had an ex-wife to get out of his system.

Tilly had forgotten Lisa for a while, but now she remembered the way Campbell had talked about her. He might not love Lisa any more, but there was definitely some unresolved business there, and Tilly had no intention of being a distraction until he found out what he really wanted. She had been that for Olivier, and she wasn't doing it again.

'I don't think that would work,' she told Campbell, choosing her words carefully.

'Because…?'

'Because we're too different. Last night was wonderful, but perhaps it was wonderful because it was just one night,' she tried to explain. 'We both got what we needed without having to think about the consequences.'

Campbell eyed her thoughtfully. 'Did we? What did you get?'

'I got Olivier out of my system,' she told him, lifting her

chin slightly. It was the truth, but not the whole truth, as they said. 'My friends have had this theory that I'd never get over him properly until I had a fling with someone to restore my confidence. And I've done that now,' she finished.

There was a tiny pause. 'I'm glad I was able to help,' said Campbell with a touch of acid.

'You know what I mean,' said Tilly. 'I mean, come on, Campbell, you know I'm right. You're leaving the country, we've got completely different lives. How could it ever be more than a night?'

All right, maybe she *was* right, thought Campbell. The trouble was that it didn't *feel* right. It felt all wrong.

But what could he do? He could hardly force her to go with him. He wasn't sure where the idea that she could go to the States with him had come from. The truth was that he had been almost as surprised by his suggestion as Tilly had been. The words seemed to have come from nowhere, and yet once they were out, they made perfect sense and Campbell had been taken aback by how badly he'd wanted Tilly to agree, how disappointed he had been when she'd said no.

Of course she was right. There was no way it could work. It was madness to even think about it. He would leave here and go to his new life in the States, and he would be grateful then that she had saved them both a lot of awkwardness by rejecting his impulsive offer.

'OK,' he admitted, 'you're right. It was just a night, but it was a great one.'

Smiling, Tilly relaxed back against the pillows. 'Yes, it was,' she said softly, 'and now you've brought breakfast, it's a wonderful morning.'

'Then let's make the most of it,' said Campbell, leaning across the tray to kiss her. 'It's not over yet.'

That had been a mistake, too, he realised much later as he watched the taxi draw up outside the house.

Had they really thought making love again would make it easier to say goodbye? Breakfast had been ruined, of course, but neither of them had cared. They had made fresh coffee eventually and reheated the croissants and ate them together, neither of them wanting to think about the minutes ticking away.

Now the moment they had both been dreading all morning had arrived.

Tilly came outside to the taxi with him. She watched as he threw his bag into the back and then turned to her.

'Well, I guess this is it,' he said.

'Yes.' Her throat tightened painfully. 'But I'll see you at the ceremony when they announce the winners. You are coming back for that, aren't you?'

'Of course,' he said, thinking that was not for another three months.

Once he would have been impatient to find out whether he had won. Now all he could think was that it meant three months without Tilly.

And, after that, the rest of his life without her.

It would be fine, he told himself. Once he was in New York, there would be so much to do, he wouldn't have time to miss her. He would be making a new life, being even more successful than before. He would be relieved that Tilly had been sensible.

He wouldn't feel the way he did now.

He looked for the last time into Tilly's dark, beautiful blue eyes, knowing that he could never tell her how he felt. So he reached for her instead, and she melted into him and they kissed, a bittersweet kiss that went on and on because neither could bear to let the other go.

'I'm glad Keith pushed me into taking part in this stupid programme,' Campbell confessed against her hair at last. 'I'm glad Greg broke his leg.'

'I'm glad you were the one who got to push me down that cliff,' said Tilly.

'I'm glad about last night, too.'

Tilly was terribly afraid that she was going to cry. She couldn't do that, not after being so brave all morning. 'Me, too.' She swallowed, hard. 'Now, get in that taxi and go before I start getting all sloppy!'

'All right,' said Campbell.

He held her tight against him for one last hard kiss and then he let her go. 'Goodbye, Jenkins. Don't go fulfilling any more fantasies without me.'

Tilly's determined smile wobbled. 'Don't call me Jenkins,' she managed with difficulty.

Her heart was cracking, tearing, as she watched him get into the taxi. 'Goodbye,' she said, but it was barely more than a whisper.

Campbell leant forward to tell the driver to take him to the station, then he looked back at Tilly and lifted a hand in farewell. She waved back, barely able to see through her tears, and then the taxi was pulling away, turning on to the street, and he was gone.

Tilly took a fortifying gulp of champagne. She probably shouldn't have ordered a glass in her room, but she badly needed something to steady her nerves. In a few minutes, she would have to go downstairs and see Campbell again, and she had no idea how she was going to handle it. For three months now, she had longed to see him, but now the moment was almost upon her she was terrified that she would simply go to pieces.

The programme had been screened the week before. Suzy

had done a good job and it had been very cleverly edited, with a fair balance between all the contestants at each stage and good coverage of their chosen charities.

Expecting it to be hidden in the daytime schedule somewhere, Tilly had been taken aback at how popular the programme had proved, and she had been overwhelmed at how many viewers had voted. Perfect strangers had come up to her in the street and told her that they hoped she would win, and the hospice had reported a flood of donations since they had been featured.

Tonight was the final ceremony when they would announce the winners, and the charities who would receive the winning donations. Tilly knew she ought to be nervous about the results, but all she could think about was seeing Campbell.

It had been three months. Three months of telling herself it was all for the best. Three months of trying to forget the night they had spent together.

Three months of missing him.

'That's what comes of forcing people out of their ruts,' she had raged to her brothers. 'I was perfectly happy until you made me do that stupid television programme.'

'We were only trying to help you get over Olivier,' they protested.

'Well, don't help any more!'

The kitchen was so empty without Campbell, her bed so lonely. It wasn't just a physical ache either. Tilly hadn't realised how alive she had felt in his presence, how everything had seemed to click into place when he'd been there. She missed talking to him, arguing with him, laughing with him... She even missed being exasperated by him. That was how bad it was.

Time and again, she'd tried to convince herself that she didn't really know Campbell at all. They had spent a matter of days together. She knew nothing about his life, his home, his friends. It was silly to build one night into such a huge deal. Much better to treat it as the brief fling she had insisted it was.

But deep down, she was convinced that she *did* know him. She knew the way the crease at the corner of his mouth deepened when he was amused. She knew exactly how he turned his head, how his brows contracted, the way he would look at her and shake his head in exasperated disbelief. There had been so many times when she'd wanted to turn to him and tell him her thoughts, and she'd always known exactly how he would reply—usually irritably, of course, but Tilly wouldn't have cared if only he had been there to reply for himself.

All the participants had been sent a copy of the final programme in advance. Tilly had watched it with Cleo and Tony, although she'd longed to be able to see it on her own so that she could freeze the picture whenever Campbell was on the screen.

Most of the shots were of the two of them together. There she was, clutching Campbell's neck at the top of that wretched cliff, falling on to the muddy river bank, playing the fool on the mountain top.

Tilly's throat had ached as she'd watched herself. She remembered it all so clearly. She could practically smell the air and feel the breeze in her face. It was as if Campbell were still beside her, making her tingle with the astringency of his presence, the touch of his hand, the heart-twisting quiver of amusement at the corner of his mouth.

There were clips from the video diaries, too. She rambled and Campbell was cool and concise. Everyone laughed at Campbell in the pink apron, but the most telling scene was at Cleo and Tony's wedding when the camera caught Tilly looking at Campbell with her heart in her eyes.

Cleo had turned and fixed her with an accusing expression. 'Why didn't you tell me you were in love with him?' she demanded.

Tilly squirmed, but couldn't deny it. 'Because there's no point in loving him,' she tried to explain. 'Nothing's going to change. Campbell's living in the States now. Even if his ex-wife doesn't want him, there'll be any number of single women in New York waiting to snap him up.'

'You should tell him how you feel,' said Cleo, but Tilly shook her head.

'It's too late for that.'

She had heard from Suzy that Campbell would only be in the country for a couple of nights. He would come to the awards ceremony, but then he had some important meeting to get back to. They wouldn't have time to do more than say hello. There was no use expecting anything else.

That didn't stop Tilly from hoping, of course. Oh, she wasn't stupid. She knew nothing lasting could come of it, but that one night had been so special, she couldn't help wanting it again. If Campbell was still single, she had decided, she was going to suggest it to him. She was staying in the hotel where the ceremony was taking place. She would have a room, if he wanted to share it with her.

CHAPTER TEN

JUST one more night. Was that so much to ask?

Tilly didn't think it was, but she wasn't sure she would have the nerve to suggest it. She had been hoping the champagne would give her Dutch courage, but it didn't seem to have had much effect yet.

Draining the glass, she put it down on the dressing table with a sharp click and regarded her reflection for a doubtful moment. She was flushed with a mixture of excitement, champagne and nerves. Her hair tumbled to her shoulders, her eyes were dark and dubious.

Cleo had insisted that she buy a new dress, and Tilly was glad now that she had. It was a lovely midnight-blue, in a flattering cut that left her shoulders bare. She picked up a gossamer-fine shawl spangled with sequins and draped it over them. She was going to feel vulnerable enough asking Campbell to make love to her one last time without feeling half naked while she did it.

After all the agony of waiting, Tilly dithered so long getting ready that she was one of the last to arrive in the ballroom where the ceremony was to take place. There was to be a champagne reception first, followed by dinner, and then some excerpts from the programme would be screened before the final winners were announced. All the participants would be there, along with representatives from the charities they supported, and Suzy had promised a good turnout from the celebrities who had been invited, too.

The room was crowded by the time Tilly arrived, but she had eyes for only one man.

Hesitating in the doorway, she let her eyes travel slowly around until they locked with a pair of familiar green ones, and her heart seemed to collide with something hard and unyielding as all the oxygen was sucked instantly from the huge room.

Campbell.

He looked amazing. He was wearing a dinner jacket that only made him look leaner, tougher and more devastating than ever.

Unsmiling, Campbell walked towards her. 'You're late, Jenkins,' he said, and then he smiled into her eyes. 'But you look wonderful.'

Tilly stammered some reply. She wanted to throw her arms round him and pat him all over like a dog to make sure he was real. Had he really said she looked wonderful?

She should ask him now, in case he had meant it, and before her mascara smudged and her lipstick wore off and she spilt something down the front of her dress. *Would you like to come to my room later?* she could say and get the question out of the way, but she hesitated too long. Maybe it *was* a bit crass to come straight out with it, before they had even had a token conversation.

The trouble was that it was difficult to have any kind of conversation when she was overwhelmed by his nearness. There was so much she wanted to ask him, so much to say, but Tilly was tongue-tied with nerves, and when a waiter passed with a tray of champagne she grabbed a glass and practically downed it in one.

'Aren't you drinking?' she asked Campbell, seeing that he was holding a glass of orange juice.

'Not yet.'

'Keeping a clear head for your winning speech?'

The dent at the corner of his mouth deepened. 'Something like that.'

There was a pause.

'So…how are you?' Tilly tried to get things going again.

'Good. And you?'

'Oh, fine, fine,' she lied. 'Is the new job going well?'

Campbell nodded. 'I'd say so. We're poised to win back a major contract, and if we can pull that off, then we should be able to start turning things round. Unfortunately, the meeting is on Monday, so I'll have to fly back tomorrow.'

'It must be important.'

'It is. It could be make or break.'

'For you or for the company?'

'Both,' said Campbell.

Tilly looked around the crowded ballroom. 'It's a long way to come for one night,' she commented.

'Some things are worth coming a long way for.'

Winning would always be worth the effort for competitive types like Campbell, Tilly remembered. 'Beating Roger and his GPS?' she enquired, and he smiled then.

'Not just that,' he said.

Tilly wanted to ask what else would matter enough to him to make it worth crossing the Atlantic for a night, two at best, but before she had a chance they were joined by Maggie, director of the hospice. She had been invited with some of the nursing staff and representatives of patients' families, and they were all much more excited about the result than Tilly was.

'You both came over wonderfully,' Maggie told them, talking about the programme. 'I do hope you'll win, and not just for what it will mean to us. Thank you so much for everything you did, especially you, Tilly.'

'That's what I always want to say to you,' said Tilly, embarrassed. 'I'll never forget what everyone at the hospice did for Mum, and for Jack. Besides, the competition turned out to be fun, so I got more out of it than anyone. I loved every minute of it.'

Campbell arched a brow. 'What, even the abseil?'

'Well, not those few minutes,' she said, making a face at him, 'but just about everything else.'

I loved being with you, she wanted to tell him, but there never seemed to be an opportunity. People kept coming up and saying how much they had enjoyed the programme. Keith, Campbell's old PR Director, ribbed him about the pink apron, Suzy wanted to talk about what would happen when the winners were announced... Couldn't they see she just wanted to be alone with Campbell?

Tilly was so jittery with frustration and nerves that she didn't notice quite how often her glass was being refilled until the wooziness hit her with a vengeance. She was badly in need of some food to mop up the champagne, but it was already half past nine and there was no sign of dinner.

She had better try and clear her head a little or she would never make it through to the announcement of the winners.

Murmuring an excuse, Tilly slipped outside. The night air was cool and quiet after the hubbub of the ballroom and she took a deep breath. How was she ever going to get Campbell on his own with all these people around? Perhaps part of her had hoped that he would follow her, but there was no sign of him. Instead, she saw Jim, the cameraman, sneaking out for a smoke.

Jim was a chatty type and, if he noticed her, he would be bound to come over and talk. It wasn't that Tilly disliked him, but there was only one man she wanted with her right then, and she made a show of digging out her mobile as if she was about to make an important call.

Out of the corner of her eye, she saw Jim veer away but,

having got that far, she thought she might as well switch the phone on. Cleo had said that she would text her to wish her luck, and Seb and Harry might remember what a big night it was for her, too.

Sure enough, there was a text message from Cleo, and another informing her that she had a message on her voicemail. Feeling virtuous without a glass of champagne in her hand, Tilly dialled up the service to listen.

It was Harry, and all thoughts of champagne were promptly driven from her mind. Horrified, she listened to his message and looked wildly round, instinctively seeking Campbell.

Campbell saw her hurry back into the ballroom and one look at her face had him striding towards her. 'What is it?' he asked sharply.

Tilly grabbed at him. 'Oh, thank goodness I've found you! It's Seb,' she said, her voice threaded with panic. 'I've just had a message from Harry. There's been an accident and Seb's in hospital… Harry said something about operating and needing me as next of kin.'

Her eyes were huge as she stared up at him. 'I don't know what to do. I know I should stay for the hospice, but I need to go to Seb. What if he's really hurt? What if he's…?'

Her voice broke, unable to finish the sentence, and Campbell gripped her firmly by both arms. 'Tell me exactly what Harry said,' he said, and Tilly drew a steadying breath as she felt the strength of his hands holding her, calming her, sending reassurance seeping through her.

'Listen to his message,' she said, holding out the phone, and Campbell put it to his ear. Harry was rambling rather than incoherent. He sounded shaken, but not desperate, and he had even ended by telling Tilly she wasn't to worry. Campbell almost smiled at that bit. Harry clearly didn't know his sister very well. There was no way Tilly wasn't going to worry after a message like that.

'Which hospital does he mean?' he asked her, hoping to get her to focus on details rather than the unknown.

'The local one in Allerby. They were both back this weekend to see friends. There was some party...' Tilly ran her hands distractedly through her hair. 'They'll all have been out playing the fool...you know what boys that age are like.'

'How are you going to get back?' Campbell asked and she looked at him, grateful that he wasn't going to waste time trying to dissuade her.

'I suppose it's too late to get a train... It'll take too long to get to the station from here. I'll have to drive,' she decided wildly. 'I'll hire a car.'

'You've been drinking.'

'Taxi, then,' she said with a touch of desperation.

'I'll drive you,' said Campbell. 'I've got a car for the couple of days I'm here, and I've been on orange juice all evening. You go and get your things.'

She stared at him, longing to put herself in his capable hands but horribly aware that she shouldn't. She should be looking after herself.

'You can't,' she said, fresh problems rearing their ugly heads. 'What about the announcement?'

'I'll explain to Maggie. If we win, she can accept the cheque for us. This whole thing has been about the hospice anyway, so I can't see there'll be a problem. I'll have a word with Suzy, too.'

'But it'll take hours to drive to Allerby from here!' With a strangely detached part of her mind, Tilly noticed that she was actually wringing her hands. 'You'll never get back in time for your flight tomorrow.'

'There will be other flights,' Campbell said.

'What about your meeting, though? You said it was really important.'

'It's not as important as getting you to Seb. Now, I'm not

going to tell you not to worry,' he went on without giving her time to react, 'but you don't need to panic. We'll get on our way and you can ring Harry and find out what's happening. You'll feel better when you've got more information.'

Tilly let herself be persuaded. She knew she shouldn't be relying on Campbell like this, but he was exactly what she needed. He was calm and competent and he was going to take her to Seb.

He dealt with all the practicalities, which meant that all she had to do was to bundle her things into her bag and hurry down to where he had the car already waiting. In a fever to get to the hospital, she hadn't even taken the time to change and was still in her blue ball gown.

At first, Tilly sat rigidly staring ahead, too tense to think about anything except what might be waiting for her at the hospital, but, as the miles passed, she gradually succumbed to the quiet reassurance of Campbell's presence and leant back inch by inch until she could relax into the luxurious leather seat.

Only then did she let herself think about the man beside her. Campbell hadn't wasted time changing either. Like most men, the severe lines of a dinner jacket suited him beautifully. Tilly eyed his profile from under her lashes, and something about the angle of his cheek made her ache.

Be careful what you wish for. Wasn't that the saying? She had longed to be alone with him, and now here they were, driving through the dark in the quiet, powerful car, but she was too consumed by anxiety to be able to say any of the things she had wanted to say to him. There would be no invitation to her room, no last night of passion, no kiss goodbye.

Tilly's heart twisted at the opportunity lost, but then she immediately felt guilty. How could any of that matter when Seb was injured?

Campbell's car was fast and comfortable and he drove it the

way he did everything else, with an austere competence and utter control. He let Tilly sit quietly when she wanted to, and when she wanted to talk about her brothers, he listened.

'They were always trouble, even as little boys,' she remembered with a wobbly smile. 'It's not that they're bad boys. They can be lovely, but they can be thoughtless and irresponsible like a lot of young men, too, and they egg each other on, just the way they used to do when they were toddlers.

'You'd think they'd be growing out of it now.' She sighed. 'They're twenty. I keep hoping they'll settle down when they graduate and have to get jobs...' Tilly trailed off as she remembered that Seb might never graduate and fear clutched at her afresh.

'It's not just Seb I'm frightened for,' she confessed in a low voice. 'It's Harry, too. They've always been so close. If anything happens to Seb...' She swallowed hard. 'Harry won't be able to bear it, I know he won't.'

She was twisting her fingers in her lap, and Campbell reached out and covered them with one big, warm hand. It felt incredibly reassuring.

'Harry will be with Seb now,' he said. 'His phone will have to be switched off in the hospital, and that's why you can't get through, but at least that means they're together.'

Tilly often wondered afterwards how she would have got through that night without Campbell. He was a fast driver, but even so it took over four hours to get to the hospital. They stopped once to fill the car up, and he bought her some coffee and chocolate biscuits, which steadied her a little, and he didn't try to tell her everything would be all right.

When they finally drew up outside the hospital, he let Tilly out so that she could run inside while he found somewhere to park. They still hadn't been able to contact Harry, and Campbell hoped he would be there or Tilly would be frantic with worry about him, too.

Fortunately, Harry was where he was supposed to be for once. Campbell eventually tracked Tilly down to a waiting area linking three wards, and found her sitting with her brother on the kind of rigid seats he always associated with airport departure lounges—the ones specially designed to discourage you from getting comfortable at all, let alone lying down.

Tilly was looking crumpled and tear-stained, but she jumped up when she saw Campbell and came instinctively towards him with her hands held out.

Campbell gripped them between his own, afraid of what the tear stains might mean. 'Seb?' he asked tensely.

'He's going to be OK.' Tilly pulled her hands away so that she could search for a tissue. 'He's sleeping, but I've seen him, and the nurse said everything went well. I'm so relieved, I can't stop crying. It's stupid, isn't it?'

'Here,' said Campbell, producing a clean handkerchief, and she took it with a watery smile and blew her nose.

'Thank you,' she said gratefully.

'Tell me what happened.'

'I haven't heard the full story yet, but it sounds as if they were all messing around at some party, and walking along walls. Seb fell badly, and broke his arm and his ankle, which will teach you not to be so silly,' she added with a darkling glance at Harry. 'It's lucky you're not both in hospital!'

Belatedly realising what all the crying must have done to her make-up, Tilly used the handkerchief to wipe under her eyes. Sure enough, it came away with great black streaks. Now not only did she look like a panda, but she had ruined Campbell's handkerchief.

'Apparently his arm had a particularly nasty fracture, so they had to reset it under anaesthetic, but he should be fine.'

'I *told* you not to worry,' said Harry defensively. He turned to Campbell. 'I can't believe she dragged you all the way up here! Seb'll be furious when he finds out.'

'It was no problem.' Campbell intervened quickly before a full-blown argument developed. 'I was glad to help.'

'I'm afraid it *was* a problem,' Tilly said ruefully when Harry had gone off to pass on the good news about Seb, and probably to continue partying, as she had observed with a sigh.

'You've missed the ceremony, your flight and your meeting,' she reminded Campbell. 'I feel terrible now. I've dragged you all the way up here for a broken arm! I'm so sorry,' she said, scrubbing absently at her face with the handkerchief. 'I should have found out more before I panicked.'

Too tired to think what to do next, Tilly dropped back down on to the bench seating under a framed print of some anonymous seaside scene. Someone had done their best, but it was a depressing place. A selection of tired-looking magazines lay on the low table with a couple of discarded plastic cups of coffee from the vending machine down the hall. At this hour of the night, the wards around them were quiet, the lighting dim.

After a moment, Campbell sat down beside her. 'You needed to be here,' he said, 'and I needed to be with you.'

'You had much more important things to do,' she said, balling the handkerchief between her hands, but Campbell shook his head.

'No,' he said, his voice quiet and firm. 'Nothing could be more important than this.'

Tilly looked at him then, her eyes dark and blue and puzzled, and something she read in his expression made her heart begin to thud.

He was tall and solid and *close* beside her and, despite her exhaustion, the receding anxiety about Seb was being replaced by a breathless awareness of Campbell, who had driven through the night for her, who had been there for her when she'd needed him.

She looked around the waiting area, at the discarded cups and uncomfortable seats. Her dress was creased and crumpled and there was a stain down the front where she must have spilt some coffee in the car. The champagne she had drunk what seemed like a lifetime ago had left her with a dull headache. Wiping the handkerchief under her eyes once more, Tilly sighed.

'This wasn't how I imagined tonight.'

'What did you think it would be like?' Campbell asked her quietly. He wasn't touching her, but she could feel his eyes on her face.

'I thought we'd be drinking champagne with a lot of glamorous people,' she said, not looking at him. 'I bought this dress specially.' She rubbed at the stain with a rueful expression. 'I wanted to look nice. I imagined us listening for the winners to be announced together, hearing our names and going up to collect the cheque for the hospice.' She smiled wistfully. 'I thought it would be great.'

'It would have been,' Campbell agreed.

Tilly nodded slowly. 'And then I imagined us celebrating together,' she went on, and she turned her head to look straight into his eyes while she told him the truth.

'I was going to suggest we go to my room so we could be alone,' she told him. 'I was going to tell you I hadn't been able to stop thinking about the night before you left. I was going to ask if we could spend one last night together.'

Campbell was sitting very still, staring at her, and she bit her lip. She might as well know the truth. 'What would you have said?'

A smile had started at the back of his eyes, giving her hope, so she wasn't expecting his answer. 'I would have said no,' he said.

'Oh.'

Tilly looked blindly away, a stricken expression in her dark blue eyes.

Very gently, Campbell reached out and laid his fingers along her jaw, turning her head back to make her face him again.

'I would have said no, I didn't want it to be a last night,' he told her softly. 'I'd have said I didn't want to say goodbye the next morning, the way we did before. If we were going to spend the night together, Tilly—and you have no idea how much I wanted that!—I wanted it to be a beginning for us, not an ending.'

Unable to speak, still reeling from that 'no', Tilly could only stare uncomprehendingly at him, and he smiled crookedly.

'This isn't how I imagined this evening either, Tilly,' he said. 'The reason I wasn't drinking earlier was because I was nervous.'

She found her voice at that. 'You? Nervous? I don't believe it!'

'It's true. But it wasn't about whether we won or not. I didn't fly all this way to hear whether the viewers thought my cake was worth more than Roger's GPS. I came to tell you that I've missed you.'

His voice was very deep as he released her face, tossed the handkerchief she was still clutching aside and took both her hands in his warm grasp.

'I came to tell you that I've thought about you every day. There I was in New York, living in a penthouse, surrounded by everything I could possibly want, and all I could think about was you, and how I wished you were there with me.

'I thought about that last night we had, too, Tilly,' he went on. 'I kept remembering what you said about it just being a fling to get over Olivier. You were so definite about us having different lives and not wanting part of mine, and I told myself that I had to respect that, but then they sent me the advance tape of the programme.'

He paused, remembering. 'I watched you on the screen, and you were so gorgeous and funny and I saw myself and it was blindingly obvious that I'd wanted you right from the start. It made me realise that I had to try and persuade you to change your mind.

'You weren't the only one with plans to say something tonight,' he told Tilly with a half smile. 'All I could think about was getting you alone somehow so I could tell you how I felt. I was going to tell you that I love you and need you, that life's no fun without you now. I was going to ask you to marry me,' said Campbell. 'Is it any wonder I was nervous?'

Tilly was struggling to take it all in. This had to be a dream, she thought. That would explain everything. She had drunk too much champagne and fallen asleep and any minute now she would wake up and her heart would break to realise that none of it was real.

But Campbell *seemed* real. This awful waiting room seemed real, and so did the biscuit crumbs in her skirt and the unmistakable hospital smell.

'If I had had the chance to say all that, Tilly, if I had been able to ask you to marry me,' said Campbell quietly, 'what would *you* have said?'

Maybe it *was* real. Tilly's heart quivered, ballooning with hope, and her eyes were huge as she looked back at him. If this were a dream, this was the point when she would fling her arms around him, laughing with delight, when she would tell him that she loved him, too, and that of course she would marry him.

But if it wasn't, if this was real after all, she would have to remember all the real reasons she hadn't told him that she loved him before.

'I think,' she said slowly at last, 'that I would have asked you if you were sure that you were over your ex-wife.'

Campbell nodded. 'That would have been a good question,' he said seriously. 'I saw Lisa in New York. I needed to see her again.'

His fingers twined around Tilly's, warm and strong. 'I hated it when she left me, but you made me realise that I hated losing more than I hated losing *her*. We weren't right together, and I know now that was as much my fault as hers.'

He paused, wondering how to explain the relief of meeting Lisa and realising that he felt nothing. 'Lisa's happy now. She's found someone who's right for her, and I'm glad for her. I wish in lots of ways that I'd faced up to seeing her again, but maybe I needed to meet you before I could understand that she did the right thing when she walked away. You taught me a lot.'

'Me?' Tilly was astonished. 'I only taught you how to make a sponge cake! I don't know how to do anything else.'

'You know more than that,' said Campbell. 'You're the one who taught me that success isn't always about what you have, or what you achieve. It's about how you live your life. You've always known that. You look after your brothers and you care for your friends, and they love you in return. You live where you want, doing a job you enjoy. You do what's right, and you do it with warmth and laughter. In the things that matter, you're the most successful person I know, Tilly.'

Tilly gulped, tried to speak and failed utterly. Nobody had ever said anything like that to her before.

Smiling at her expression, Campbell tightened his hold on her hand. 'So, no, this isn't how I imagined tonight,' he said. 'I imagined I would tell you all of that without making a fool of myself, or stumbling and stuttering too much when I asked you to marry me. I'd even let myself imagine you'd say yes.'

His smile twisted. 'I thought we would be in bed by now, loving each other, instead of which we're sitting here in this crummy waiting room, and you're tired and worried and we're both miles away from where we should be, but I don't care. I don't care what happens as long as I'm with you.'

Tilly's heart was beating so loudly by then that she was afraid it was going to burst right through her ribs. She so badly wanted to believe him…but how could she?

'But look at me,' she said helplessly. 'I'm a mess! I'm fat and piggy-eyed and my hair's a disaster and my dress is ruined!'

'You're not a mess,' he said. 'You're beautiful.'

'Don't make fun of me!'

'I'm not. God, Tilly, you have the self-confidence of a shrimp!' said Campbell, sounding almost his old exasperated self. 'Who cares if your dress is creased or your mascara's run? You're still gorgeous. Why won't you believe me?'

'Because…' Tilly gestured helplessly.

'Because that moron Olivier convinced you you weren't thin enough or smart enough or perfectly groomed enough for him?'

'I suppose so,' she muttered.

'And because your father made you think the same thing when you were just a little girl?'

'Probably.' She wouldn't meet his eyes.

'Come here,' said Campbell, pulling her on to his lap and holding her firmly with one arm while his free hand smoothed her hair away from her face. 'Do you remember that abseil?'

'Yes,' said Tilly cautiously, not quite ready to believe him, but wrapping her arms around his neck anyway. It seemed rude not to and, anyway, what else could she do with them when she was trapped on his lap like this?

'You didn't trust me then,' he reminded her. 'You begged me not to let you go.'

'I was terrified!'

'*Did* I let you go?'

'No,' she admitted.

'Did I tell you you could make it to the top of that mountain?'

'You did.'

'And was I right?'

A smile tugged at Tilly's mouth. 'I see where you're going with this,' she told him.

'Go on, admit it.' He grinned. 'I was right.'

She rolled her eyes. 'Yes, you were right.'

'I'm right about this, too,' said Campbell, and his smile

faded. 'You're gorgeous and sexy and warm and funny and I adore you and, if you'll marry me, I'll spend the rest of my life trying to make you happy.'

And then, because talking didn't seem to be getting him anywhere fast, he kissed her.

Tilly was lost the moment their lips met and she sank into him, giving back kiss for kiss, while happiness poured like liquid sunshine along her veins. 'I love you,' she confessed, mumbling between kisses. 'I love you, I love you.'

'At last!' Campbell pretended to grumble, holding her hard against him. 'I thought I was never going to get you to say it! *Now* will you marry me?'

'Do you promise not to let me go?'

'I promise,' he said gravely.

'In that case, I will,' she said, and he kissed her again.

'It's lucky you said that,' Campbell said when he came up for air at last. He dug around in the inside pocket of his jacket. 'I can give you this now.'

He produced a little box. 'I promised you roses once if we got through the competition,' he reminded her, 'but I'm hoping you might like this instead.'

Tilly's eyes widened, and he watched anxiously as she opened the box and drew a sharp gasp. Nestled in the velvet padding was a band of exquisite diamonds bracketing a deep, square-cut sapphire.

'It's the colour of your eyes,' he said.

For a long moment Tilly couldn't say anything. Her heart was too full to speak, and her eyes when she lifted them to his were shimmering with tears. 'Campbell…' was all she could manage.

The tears made Campbell nervous. 'Maybe you would rather choose it yourself?' he said hurriedly. 'We can change it if you want.'

'No.' Tilly stopped him with a kiss. 'It's perfect,' she told him with a shaky smile. 'I'm only crying because I'm so happy.'

Campbell let himself relax a little. 'Are you sure you like it?'

'I love it…almost as much as I love you, in fact!'

'Try it on.' Picking up the ring, he made Tilly hold out her left hand.

'I hope it's not too small,' she said, bracing herself for humiliation, but it slid on to her finger as if made for it. 'Oh, Campbell, it's beautiful,' she told him, her eyes starry as she kissed him again. 'Now I know you really *do* want to marry me,' she said. 'You had it planned down to the last detail!'

Campbell laughed with relief as he pulled her close. 'It didn't work out exactly as I'd planned, or we would be somewhere a lot more comfortable than this where I could make love to you the way I've been thinking about making love to you for the past three months.'

Tilly allowed herself a last kiss and slid off his knee. 'In that case,' she said, 'I think we should go home.'

'I was thinking I could give up my job in the States and come back here,' said Campbell as they walked down the quiet hospital corridors. 'I know you're happy here in Allerby, and I could find another role somewhere round here.'

Tilly thought about it while they waited for a lift. 'No,' she decided eventually. 'Not unless you have to find another job after missing that meeting!'

'I'm not going to miss it,' he said confidently. 'I'll get myself back there in time for it somehow, and then I'll come back and be with you.'

'I think I should go to you,' said Tilly. 'Harry and Seb have been going on at me to get out of my rut, so that's what I'll do,' she said bravely. 'I can make cakes in America as well as here.'

They walked hand in hand across the silent hospital grounds

to where Campbell had left his car. 'I'm nervous about the idea of a penthouse, though,' she admitted. 'I bet it's immaculate.'

He smiled down at her. 'We can buy a messy house if you like.'

'It's not the house, it's the kind of life you live.' Tilly hesitated, chewing her lip. 'I think I might be losing my nerve already! We're so different.' She looked anxiously at him. 'Do you really think if we get married we'll live happily ever after?'

Campbell stopped and turned to face her. 'I don't know,' he said honestly. 'We're bound to argue about stuff, and maybe things will be difficult sometimes, but we'll have to work it out together.'

Pulling her in to him, he rested his cheek against her hair. 'There are no guarantees, Tilly, but if you love me and I love you, and if we trust each other, I think we'll make it. I know it's a risk, but this time,' he said, 'we're going over the cliff together.'

Tilly smiled as she remembered that first morning and how terrified she had been at the end of that rope. What was it she had said to him then? She pulled back slightly so she could put her arms around his neck and draw his head down for a kiss warm with promise.

'Let's get on with it then,' she said.

Enveloped in a haze of delight, they were almost back at the house before they remembered the competition. Tilly switched on her phone to find a message from Suzy, the producer.

'Oh,' she said, and glanced at Campbell, hoping he wasn't going to be too disappointed. 'Apparently it was very close, but Roger and Leanne won in the end. There's a message from Maggie, too...'

She listened closely, then closed the phone. 'Maggie says she's really sorry we didn't win, but she wants to thank you for matching the winner's cheque with a donation to the hospice.'

Reaching across, she laid a hand on his thigh and smiled. 'That was generous of you.'

Campbell drew up outside Tilly's house and switched off the engine. 'For the record, I would have done it for Roger and Leanne's charities as well if we'd won,' he said with a shrug. 'The competition was just to make the programme more interesting for the viewers. I didn't want any of those good causes to miss out on money that could make a real difference.'

Leaning across the handbrake, he kissed her. 'I even arranged a donation to mountain rescue dog training.'

'Whatever for?'

'It turns out that was Greg's chosen charity, and I felt it was the least I owed him for breaking his leg and making it possible for me to meet you. It seems a bit unfair on the poor bloke, but I'll always be glad that he did!'

Tilly laughed as she got out of the car, but her expression was doubtful as they walked to the front door. 'Are you *sure* you don't mind that we didn't win?'

But Campbell, Mr Competitive, only smiled and put an arm around her. 'I'm here with you and we've got the rest of our lives together,' he said simply. 'I think we *are* the winners, don't you?'

When he put it like that, Tilly could only agree. Smiling, she found her keys and unlocked the door. 'Much as I hate to admit it, I think you're right about that, too!'

* * * * *

Here's a sneak peek at
THE CEO'S CHRISTMAS PROPOSITION,
the first in USA TODAY *bestselling author Merline*
Lovelace's HOLIDAYS ABROAD *trilogy coming in*
November 2008.

American Devon McShay is about to get the Christmas
surprise of a lifetime when she meets her new client,
sexy billionaire Caleb Logan, for the very first time.

Silhouette

Desire

Available November 2008

Her breath whistled out in a sigh of relief when he exited Customs. Devon recognized him right away from the newspaper and magazine articles her friend and partner Sabrina had looked up during her frantic prep work.

Caleb John Logan, Jr. Thirty-one. Six-two. With jet-black hair, laser-blue eyes and a linebacker's shoulders under his charcoal-gray cashmere overcoat. His jaw-dropping good looks didn't score him any points with Devon. She'd learned the hard way not to trust handsome heartbreakers like Cal Logan.

But he was a client. An important one. And she was willing to give someone who'd served a hitch in the marines before earning a B.S. from the University of Oregon, an MBA from Stanford and his first million at the ripe old age of twenty-six the benefit of the doubt.

Right up until he spotted the hot-pink pashmina, that is.

Devon knew the flash of color was more visible than the sign she held up with his name on it. So she wasn't surprised when Logan picked her out of the crowd and cut in her direction. She'd just plastered on her best businesswoman smile when he whipped an arm around her waist. The next moment she was sprawled against his cashmere-covered chest.

"Hello, brown eyes."

Swooping down, he covered her mouth with his.

Sheer astonishment kept Devon rooted to the spot for a few

seconds while her mind whirled chaotically. Her first thought was that her client had downed a few too many drinks during the long flight. Her second, that he'd mistaken the kind of escort and consulting services her company provided. Her third shoved everything else out of her head.

The man could kiss!

His mouth moved over hers with a skill that ignited sparks at a half dozen flash points throughout her body. Devon hadn't experienced that kind of spontaneous combustion in a while. A *long* while.

The sparks were still popping when she pushed off his chest, only now they fueled a flush of anger.

"Do you always greet women you don't know with a lip-lock, Mr. Logan?"

A smile crinkled the skin at the corners of his eyes. "As a matter of fact, I don't. That was from Don."

"Huh?"

"He said he owed you one from New Year's Eve two years ago and made me promise to deliver it."

She stared up at him in total incomprehension. Logan hooked a brow and attempted to prompt a nonexistent memory.

"He abandoned you at the Waldorf. Five minutes before midnight. To deliver twins."

"I don't have a clue who or what you're…"

Understanding burst like a water balloon.

"Wait a sec. Are you talking about Sabrina's old boyfriend? Your buddy, who's now an ob-gyn doc?"

It was Logan's turn to look startled. He recovered faster than Devon had, though. His smile widened into a rueful grin.

"I take it you're not Sabrina Russo."

"No, Mr. Logan, I am *not*."

* * * * *

Be sure to look for
THE CEO'S CHRISTMAS PROPOSITION
by Merline Lovelace.
Available in November 2008 wherever books are sold,
including most bookstores, supermarkets, drugstores
and discount stores.

Silhouette *Desire*

MERLINE LOVELACE

THE CEO'S CHRISTMAS PROPOSITION

After being stranded in Austria together
at Christmas, it takes only one kiss for
aerospace CEO Cal Logan to decide he wants
more than just a business relationship with
Devon McShay. But when Cal's credibility is
questioned, he has to fight to clear his name,
and to get Devon to trust her heart.

**Available November
wherever books are sold.**

Holidays Abroad

Always Powerful, Passionate and Provocative.

Visit Silhouette Books at www.eHarlequin.com   SD76905

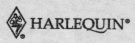

HARLEQUIN®

American ★ Romance®

Laura Marie Altom
A Daddy
for Christmas

The State of Parenthood

Single mom Jesse Cummings is struggling
to run her Oklahoma ranch and raise her
two little girls after the death of her husband.
Then on Christmas Eve, a miracle strolls onto
her land in the form of tall, handsome bull
rider Gage Moore. He doesn't plan on staying,
but in the season of miracles, anything
can happen....

***Available November
wherever books are sold.***

LOVE, HOME & HAPPINESS

www.eHarlequin.com
HAR75237

nocturne™

**ESCAPE THE CHILL OF WINTER WITH TWO SPECIAL
STORIES FROM BESTSELLING AUTHORS**

MICHELE
HAUF

AND

VIVI ANNA

WINTER KISSED

In "A Kiss of Frost," photographer Kate Wilson experiences
the icy kisses of Jal Frosti, but soon learns that this icy god
has a deadly ulterior motive. Can Kate's love melt his heart?

In "Ice Bound," Dr. Darien Calder travels to the north
island of Japan, where he discovers an icy goddess who is
rumored to freeze doomed travelers. Darien is determined
to melt her beautiful but frosty exterior and break her of
the curse she carries...before it's too late.

Available November wherever books are sold.

www.eHarlequin.com
www.paranormalromanceblog.wordpress.com   SN61799

Silhouette®

Romantic
SUSPENSE

**Sparked by Danger,
Fueled by Passion.**

Lindsay McKenna
Susan Grant

Mission: Christmas

Celebrate the holidays with a pair
of military heroines and their daring men
in two romantic, adventurous stories
from these bestselling authors.

Featuring:

"The Christmas Wild Bunch"
by *USA TODAY* bestselling author
Lindsay McKenna

and

"Snowbound with a Prince"
by *New York Times* bestselling author
Susan Grant

Available November wherever books are sold.

Visit Silhouette Books at www.eHarlequin.com   SRS27605

REQUEST YOUR FREE BOOKS!
2 FREE NOVELS PLUS 2
FREE GIFTS!

HARLEQUIN ROMANCE®

From the Heart, For the Heart

YES! Please send me 2 FREE Harlequin Romance® novels and my 2 FREE gifts (gifts are worth about $10). After receiving them, if I don't wish to receive any more books, I can return the shipping statement marked "cancel." If I don't cancel, I will receive 4 brand-new novels every month and be billed just $3.32 per book in the U.S. or $3.80 per book in Canada, plus 25¢ shipping and handling per book and applicable taxes, if any*. That's a savings of over 15% off the cover price! I understand that accepting the 2 free books and gifts places me under no obligation to buy anything. I can always return a shipment and cancel at any time. Even if I never buy another book, the two free books and gifts are mine to keep forever.

114 HDN ERQW   314 HDN ERQ9

Name	(PLEASE PRINT)	
Address		Apt. #
City	State/Prov.	Zip/Postal Code

Signature (if under 18, a parent or guardian must sign)

Mail to the **Harlequin Reader Service:**
IN U.S.A.: P.O. Box 1867, Buffalo, NY 14240-1867
IN CANADA: P.O. Box 609, Fort Erie, Ontario L2A 5X3

Not valid to current subscribers of Harlequin Romance books.

Want to try two free books from another line?
Call 1-800-873-8635 or visit www.morefreebooks.com.

* Terms and prices subject to change without notice. N.Y. residents add applicable sales tax. Canadian residents will be charged applicable provincial taxes and GST. Offer not valid in Quebec. This offer is limited to one order per household. All orders subject to approval. Credit or debit balances in a customer's account(s) may be offset by any other outstanding balance owed by or to the customer. Please allow 4 to 6 weeks for delivery. Offer available while quantities last.

Your Privacy: Harlequin Books is committed to protecting your privacy. Our Privacy Policy is available online at www.eHarlequin.com or upon request from the Reader Service. From time to time we make our lists of customers available to reputable third parties who may have a product or service of interest to you. If you would prefer we not share your name and address, please check here. ☐

HR08R

Inside ROMANCE

Stay up-to-date on all your romance reading news!

The Inside Romance newsletter is a FREE quarterly newsletter highlighting our upcoming series releases and promotions!

Click on the <u>Inside Romance</u> link on the front page of **www.eHarlequin.com** or e-mail us at insideromance@harlequin.ca to sign up to receive your FREE newsletter today!

You can also subscribe by writing us at: HARLEQUIN BOOKS
Attention: Customer Service Department
P.O. Box 9057, Buffalo, NY 14269-9057

Please allow 4-6 weeks for delivery of the first issue by mail.

IRNBPA208

HARLEQUIN *Romance*

Coming Next Month

Get into the holiday spirit this month as Harlequin Romance® brings you...

#4057 HER MILLIONAIRE, HIS MIRACLE Myrna Mackenzie
Heart to Heart
Rich and powerful Jeremy has just discovered he's going blind, and he's determined to keep his independence. Shy Eden has loved Jeremy from afar for so long. Can the woman he once overlooked persuade him to accept her help—and her love?

#4058 WEDDED IN A WHIRLWIND Liz Fielding
Miranda is on a dream tropical-island holiday when disaster strikes! She's trapped in a dark cave and is scared for her life...but worse, she's not alone! Miranda is trapped with macho adventurer Nick—and the real adventure is just about to begin....

#4059 RESCUED BY THE MAGIC OF CHRISTMAS
Melissa McClone
Carly hasn't celebrated Christmas for six years—not since her fiancé died. But this year, courageous mountain rescuer Jake is determined she'll enjoy herself and dispel her fear of loving again with the magic of Christmas.

#4060 BLIND DATE WITH THE BOSS Barbara Hannay
9 to 5
Sally has come to Sydney for a fresh start. And she's trying to ignore her attraction to brooding M.D. Logan. But when he's roped into attending a charity ball, fun-loving Sally waltzes into his life, and it will never be the same again....

#4061 THE TYCOON'S CHRISTMAS PROPOSAL Jackie Braun
With the dreaded holidays approaching, the last thing widowed businessman Dawson needs is a personal shopper who wants to get *personal*. But Eve is intent on getting him into the Christmas spirit, and she's hoping he'll give her the best Christmas present of all—a proposal!

#4062 CHRISTMAS WISHES, MISTLETOE KISSES Fiona Harper
After leaving her cheating husband, Louise is determined to make this Christmas perfect for her and her young son. But it's not until she meets gorgeous architect Ben that her Christmas really begins to sparkle....

HRCNM1008